"Cole, why did you come?"

Sheila turned her head so she knew he could see her face if he chose. "Is it because you feel sorry for me?"

"Partly," he answered curtly.

She flinched, but his response was no more than she had expected. She hadn't, however, expected the truth to cut so deeply, and she turned away toward the window, not wanting him to see how much he had hurt her.

"I said *partly* ," Cole emphasized with grating coolness. "You know the other reason—if you're brave enough to admit it."

"I thought . . . you haven't . . . oh . . . " She was as helplessly flustered as a school girl, and Cole's soft, taunting laughter only served to further disconcert her. "But . . . I'm blind!"

THROUGH A GLASS DARKLY

Sara Mitchell

Serenade/Serenata
BOOKS
of the Zondervan Publishing House
Grand Rapids, Michigan

THROUGH A GLASS DARKLY
Copyright 1985 by The Zondervan Corporation

Serenade/Serenata is an imprint of
The Zondervan Publishing House
1415 Lake Drive, S.E.
Grand Rapids, Michigan 49506

ISBN 0-310-46722-5

Edited by Anne Severance
Designed by Kim Koning

Printed in the United States of America

85 86 87 88 89 90 / 10 9 8 7 6 5 4 3 2 1

To my friends, who supported me
To my mother and husband, whose faith in me
removed mountains of doubt
To Anne, for both her faith and support . . .
and because she walks far beyond the second
mile.

"For now we see through a glass, darkly; but then face to face: now I know in part; but then shall I know even as also I am known."

I Corinthians 13:12, KJV

CHAPTER 1

'I . . . THINK THAT I SHALL NEVER SEE . . . .'' Sheila Jamison, her slender five-feet-four-inch form striking a dramatic pose center stage, paused just as dramatically, her nose wrinkling, '' . . . a boy who *QUITE* appeals to me.''

She peered down, brown eyes dancing, at a young teen-aged girl and youth minister of their church. ''See? That's what I mean. You can't perform this too slapsticky—but then you can't treat it like the Metropolitan Opera either.'' She moved lightly over to the edge of the stage and hopped down, grinning when Mike, the minister of music, put his hands over his eyes and groaned. ''Mike, I've been jumping off this stage since I was six years old in the first grade and I haven't broken anything yet.''

''There's always a first time.''

''Well, I promise not to make it the week before the annual Choir Foibles and Follies. Isn't it great that we've had to move to the school auditorium this year?'' She grabbed Angela's hands and swung around with her in an impromptu polka. ''I just wish I could sing so I could take more of a part in it.''

Mike winced openly. "My sweet girl," he intoned with mock gravity, "I thank the good Lord above for your ability to compose poetry, act, choreograph, and keep a clear if nutty head in between. But spare us the joyful but very definite noise you make when you try to sing."

All three of them laughed. Sheila's inability to carry a tune was as legendary as her zany sense of the ridiculous. "If you weren't so—oo-o right I'd be so-oo-oo hurt, Michael Murphy."

"Sheila! Hey, Sheila!" came an adolescent voice from the back of the auditorium as he bounded down the aisle. "I just came from the church, and Mrs. Allendre said to tell you she is sorry, but she couldn't find anyone to sub for you this Sunday and you'll just have to wing it." He came skidding to a halt and finished breathlessly, "or words to that effect. And I asked Skip and Doug to help with the sets and they said they'd be here by seven-thirty."

"Okay, thanks, Nat. Good going."

"Sheila, can we go over the song *once* more?" Angela begged. "I still keep missing that part about the guy keeping his shirttail in . . . ."

"Probably because I've never seen Eddie with his tucked in," Sheila replied dryly. Sheila liked him well enough, but neatness was apparently not part of his chosen lifestyle. She sighed, motioned Angela up onto the stage and, with the agility of a ten-year-old, hopped up after her, the long brown braid that spilled down her back swinging crazily from one hip to the other.

Again she went through a parody of Joyce Kilmer's famous poem, 'Trees;' her version entitled "Boys" instead, miming and over-emphasizing with Angela until the girl felt confident. Then she spent an hour with Mike, going over the script once more to make sure they had the proper sequence of events. After that, she had to check on the sets created by volunteers from the youth group.

". . . and somehow between now and Sunday morning, I have to study a Sunday school lesson for my little batch of sugar-and-spice-and snakes-and-snails . . ." she moaned late that night walking home with David Sayer, the dentist she had been dating off and on for the past few months. Her affectionate title for the group of eight-year-olds she taught sent a grin flitting across his face, and Sheila smiled ruefully back.

"You're some kind of gal, Sheila Jamison." David dropped his arm around her shoulders in an affectionate bear hug. "It's a shame that you're so wonderful I'm afraid to try and stake any claims. All your friends would put me through a baptism by fire."

"Well, I was going to reply that you were some kind of guy, but after a sappy observation like *that* I've changed my mind!" They had reached the walk that led to Sheila's front door and she moved lightly, gracefully, from beneath David's arm. "That kind of remark is enough to make even 'wonderful me' long to do something low and nasty. Something so despicable you would duck into a dark alley rather than pass by me on the street." She wrinkled her nose at him, hiding the solemnity of her dark brown eyes.

"Nut. You wouldn't know how to act venal if your life depended on it. Now come here and kiss me goodnight. It's late and I have at least twenty patients booked for tomorrow."

His arms lifted again, but Sheila forestalled the embrace by swiftly rising on tiptoes to bestow a soft kiss on his cheek.

"Goodnight, David. And thanks for the endorsement of my character."

Sheila was unnaturally pensive as she performed her bedtime ablutions. It was true she enjoyed—at times endured—the reputation of being . . . nice. Or sweet. "And full of love and laughter," she recited to herself as she settled beneath the single crisp sheet that shortly would be kicked into a rumpled mass. The nights in the small town near Roanoke, Virginia where she had lived all her life were hot in July, even though Camden was nestled in the foothills of the Shenandoah Valley. *Lord, sometimes I can't help wondering why You've blessed me so . . . health, home, friends, career . . . .* She fell asleep with a wistful, impish smile on her lips and the half-formed thought that pride went before destruction, and was thankfulness for all her blessings a form of pride? Was that why it was so easy for her to be such a 'nice person?' And what about her outrageous, irrepressible sense of humor . . . a blessing or a burden?

The next afternoon while watering some of her mother's prized shasta daisies, Sheila gazed around the yard with suddenly misty eyes. It was so beautiful, even in mid-summer when the scorching sun quickly browned anything that wasn't watered. Dad always used to complain about the water bill from May until November, but all Mom had had to do was give him one of "her looks" and Dad would have bought her the ocean if it had been for sale. How merciful God had been to take them within six months of each other, Sheila reflected, smiling a little as she wandered over to check the pansies that were prospering in the windowbox beneath the kitchen window. First Dad of a heart attack, then Mom from complications with pneumonia. She knew her parents were together now, and happy, and that knowledge had helped sustain Sheila herself through the grief . . . .

If she hadn't wandered back to check on the pansies, she would have missed the ringing of the phone that interrupted her reverie. "Hello?" she answered breathlessly, and the caller chuckled.

"Catch you out in the yard for a change, did I?"

"How did you guess?" Sheila laughed back. It was Doris Allendre, and Sheila sprawled out in a kitchen

10

chair, a pleased smile lighting her voice. Over the last five years she and Doris had grown as close as sisters, even though Doris was almost old enough to be her mother.

"Well, I won't keep you but a minute. If you're outside instead of inside, with your nose buried in your typewriter, I certainly don't want to discourage you."

"Just two months ago I found time to take a bath on Saturday night."

"Okay, okay," Doris conceded. Her friend never stopped nagging Sheila about her unconventional work habits, and Sheila always replied with the craziest comeback her agile brain could devise. This time, however, Doris would not be deterred. "Actually, this is another means to an end as far as dragging you away from the slave-driving muse that chains you—"

"I tried to hire a lazy one, but they were all taken."

"—and it is an emotional blackmail plea for you to come to Cole Hampton's annual open house with us this year."

Sheila groaned. "Doris, we've had this conversation every year for . . . four years now, I believe. You *know* how I feel about that kind of thing! I have absolutely *nothing* in common with the Hampton Electronics crowd, unless you consider my 'sizzling' personality. 'Watt' a line, huh?"

"Sheila," Doris' voice was patient, "when you crack atrocious puns, I know it's because you're nervous. But I am *begging* in behalf of my *own* nervousness. Joe and I are expected to attend, and I'm more of a fish out of water there than you would be."

"Far better to feel like an awkward fish and not talk at all than to open your mouth and insert a foot the size of a whale." Sheila wound the phone cord round and round her finger, sitting up straight in the chair

now as she frantically pleaded her own case. "Doris,
Mom vowed after we attended that formal reception
for college freshmen that she would never make that
mistake again. Or at least never be present for it
. . . ."

"Sheila, that was six years ago."

"Do you know why? I was so nervous about being
properly *formal* and correct when presented to the
president that I drank some punch too fast and gave
myself the hiccups." She took a deep breath. "Doris,
when I opened my mouth to speak to him nothing but
this horribly loud hiccup came out. I wanted to die!"

"I know how you feel." The same desperation was
in Doris' voice. "That's why you've GOT to come
this year. We can stick together and support each
other. It's the first year Joe will be considered top
brass, remember? I don't want everyone thinking his
wife is a total dud now that he's finally on the board."

"Just pretend you're talking to me—or anybody at
church. You never have a problem there."

"Very funny. But that's just it, and it's also the
reason *you* keep refusing. Our lives are so different
from these people; I don't know any of them or what
they do in their spare time . . . or even if they go to
church at all. What do I talk about?"

Sheila heaved a sigh, feeling trapped. "You could
always talk about Cole Hampton's house—or his
genius—or his women." She smiled in response to
Doris' groan. Although Sheila had never met him,
she—along with the rest of the population of south-
western Virginia—was aware of many of the pertinent statistics about Cole Hampton. A self-made
millionaire, he was president and controlling force
behind Hampton Electronics, a huge multi-complex
sprawling over several acres on the western edge of
town. A confirmed bachelor in his mid-thirties, he
liked wine, women, and work, not necessarily in that
order. There was little chance that he would be likely

12

to ever darken the doors of hers and the Allen-dres'church, and just about that much chance of Sheila darkening the doorstep of his home.

"Sheila . . . please."

There was a full minute of protracted silence.

"All right. I'll come." She capitulated with grave forboding, but her heart just couldn't harden against that quiet, ragged plea. "What's the date again?"

"Oh, thank you! THANK YOU! You just don't know . . . ." For several minutes Sheila endured her friend's rhapsodies of appreciation while a detached portion of her brain committed her body to an asylum. Doris finally ran down. " . . . and since it's this Saturday, it won't interfere with the Choir Follies on Friday. I thought we'd pick you up at—"

"Oh, Doris, not *this* Saturday!" Sheila sailed. "I promised Daniel I'd meet him at the airport in Roanoke. He's making a special detour on his way to New York, so I can give him my latest collection of poems." Excitement edged into the chagrin. "He wants to show them to a friend of his who owns a chain of department stores. The possibilities . . . . Oh, please, *please* say you understand."

"I do, Sheila. I really do. It's a tremendous opportunity for you."

There was so much genuine happiness in her voice that Sheila wanted to weep. She hadn't wanted to go to the open house, it was true, but she wanted to hurt Doris even less. "How about . . . would it . . . " she gnawed her lip, then took the plunge. "How about if I meet you and Joe there later on in the evening? I could probably make it by nine or nine-thirty, and then I promise I'd stick like a cocklebur to your side." She laughed a shaky laugh. "Although you'll probably regret it after ten minutes."

The relief flooded over the phone in waves. "Honey, if you *could* do that I don't think I'd care if you even cracked some of your awful jokes or made up your corny jingles or—or even sang!"

"Never!" Sheila exclaimed in mock horror. "Although I warn you I might be desperate enough to start impromptu poems of doubtful literary appeal. The kids in the Sunday school class love them, but I'm not so sure about that crowd."

"Silly girl . . . ." Now that she had been reassured of Sheila's agreement Doris adopted an affectionate mothering tone. "I don't know why *you* feel so awkward at formal social gatherings. I'm the frumpy one but you, Sheila—*you* light up a room with your smile."

"Hush that kind of talk. You are not a frump."

"We're talking about you, not me. You're the life of every church social, the favorite babysitter in town and I know that new dentist is besotted. Why on earth did a gal like you develop feelings of inadequacy?"

"David Sayer is a very nice man, and he is NOT besotted," Sheila mumbled. "And I'm that way because we never really entertained that much . . . and it seems like I'm cursed with this wretched little imp that hates formal situations. Every time I'm supposed to be proper and sedate, I always end up like a kid with her hand in the cookie jar and chocolate smeared on her face."

"You don't have any trouble in church services."

"That's different! That's not *formal* formal . . . that's worship." She stood up, absently flipping the braid out of the way. "Doris, I can't explain it, but church is different. It's easy there because I feel I owe God so much I sometimes want to bubble up and overflow with—with joy. But at a cocktail party, with people I don't know who are talking about other people and things I don't know , I just—" she stopped, so tangled in words and the phone cord that she lost her train of thought.

"Never mind, honey." Doris was comforting, soothing. "I understand better than you realize. I just love you all the more for bailing me out." She adopted

14

a teasing tone now. "Buy yourself a new dress, and I might even arrange for you to meet the head man himself."

"God forbid!" Sheila blurted fervently, and meant it.

They hung up a few minutes later without further mention of the dreaded open house. But Sheila went immediately back to her bedroom to the closet and stood examining its contents with a worried grimace distorting her even features. She would definitely have to buy a new dress. The pristine white lace and silk she had worn that infamous day to the president's reception held too many memories. It also looked like something a youngish eighteen-year-old would wear.

Sheila glanced down at her faded T-shirt and soiled jeans and had to laugh. She knew she didn't look a day older than that in this outfit, and most of the time she felt more of a kinship with ten-year-old Corrie Oates across the street. "What does a twenty-four-going-on-twenty-five-year-old woman with a career on the rise wear to the social event of the year?" she mused aloud.

And what, her vivid imagination puzzled at odd moments over the next several days, did her career have in common with electronics geniuses, managers-of-whatever-they-managed, secretaries, and all the other social lions and lionesses who would be present there?

She spent most of the week working on some get-well verses, forcing her energies to her work and refusing to allow more than a momentary twinge of panic. The lines of verse seemed to flow directly from her heart to the paper. The Bible, which was her primary source of inspiration, was always a veritable treasure house of comforting verses. And coming up with an appropriate poem of twenty lines or less was as easy as hopping over Mulberry Creek, which always dried up in the summer anyway.

Sheila often marveled at the satisfaction and joy she received from her rather unusual career. If someone had told her five years earlier, when she was a bubbling nineteen and planning to major in Early Childhood Education, that she would instead end up making an astonishingly profitable living writing inspirational greeting cards, she probably would have very solemnly informed them that they had been out in the sun too long. She had been making cards and writing verses to go with them since she was a child. As she grew older her mother had paid her ten cents a card whenever an occasion arose and gradually friends and relatives followed suit. She had paid for the bulk of her education that way, although the degree was lying in a drawer in the spare bedroom, unused.

The direction of her life changed dramatically after the death of her parents, and she had been forced to drop out of school for a year. To help cope with her grief and the months of uncertainty, she had designed and handwritten little cards of appreciation and acknowledgment to the friends who had shown so much love and caring during this traumatic time. One friend had shown her card to a man who owned a small publishing house in North Carolina. He, in turn, had shown it to another man who owned a regional chain of card and gift stores. Daniel Everett had personally paid her a visit, and after a week of heart-searching prayer and meditation, Sheila had accepted his offer.

Sheila finished college because it wasn't in her nature to leave anything undone, but the diploma went in the drawer and she had never looked back. God had directed her down a path of His choosing, and she would never argue with that. She had received too many blessings from Him to question His ways.

By Thursday she was through with the selection of verses dealing with illnesses and recoveries, and knew that she could not put off any longer dealing with the Saturday night that was fast approaching. Although she had prayed about it faithfully, and knew that all she had to do was trust and leave the matter in the good Lord's capable hands, she also knew that it was up to her to act on that faith, and so Thursday afternoon she went shopping for a new dress.

Sheila had never spent much time on clothes or her looks. She did not consider herself beautiful, and clothes were merely a necessary encumbrance. When she was complimented on her large brown eyes, or perhaps her sunny smile, she shrugged the words aside with a self-conscious thank you. She had the same deep convictions as her parents about inner beauty, and because it was in her nature to care about others more than herself, she had never been overly preoccupied with her own outer trappings. She was now.

Somehow it was very important not to let Doris down, and if she was confident about her appearance, maybe—just maybe she could sail in serene sophistication through the evening. Sail with confident conversation that was not sprinkled with giggles or gaffes. Sail with graciousness instead of . . . instead of the hiccups.

As she trudged in and out of stores looking for "the" dress, Sheila mentally composed and discarded ice-breakers, conversational topics, and proper etiquette. She was in the middle of muttering a prayerful plea for God to either change her whole personality— or inflict her with a very contagious disease—when she ran into Elaine Dreyfus, one of her closest friends.

Immediately sensing Sheila's distraction, Elaine took charge. She found THE dress in short order, plus a mind-boggling assortment of other 'necessary accessories,' then marched Sheila into Wilson's Drug Store and sat her down at the soda fountain, and ordered two chocolate shakes.

"Now," she eyed Sheila's frazzled braid and clean, scrubbed face as she sipped the thick drink, "we've got the outfit, so all that's left is your hair, your make-up, and your attitude."

Sheila slurped noisily, rolling her eyes in a Groucho Marx imitation. "How about two out of three? We're talking about something as drastic as Daniel being thrown in the lion's den here, remember?"

"Don't be such a ninny!" Elaine returned with exasperation. "Sheila, you're one of those rare Christians who actually live their faith instead of trying to shove it down everyone's throats. And that's why you'll be fine at Cole Hampton's open house. All you have to do is be yourself. Don't worry about offending anyone when they ask what you do and your answer is what they might deem a 'religious' one. Don't worry about what to say, or whether your mouth opens and a crazy poem falls out. That's *you*, Sheila, and everyone loves you just as you are." She gave Sheila a playful shove. "If *I* didn't love you so much, I'd be jealous of you."

"You're a friend in a million, Elaine . . . ." Sheila finished her own shake and rich, dark brown eyes met intent, sincere blue ones. "You know, Dad used to say that all the money and all the looks in the world weren't worth the peace of God. He was so right, and I see now that I just needed to be reminded of it. If the good Lord saw fit to grant me my . . . um . . . wacky personality, then it means all I can do is smile nicely and say thank you. Usually I do . . . but this is the first year Doris has managed to outwit me with that open house, and I guess I've been off balance ever since."

"You'll be the hit of it all, you'll see."

" 'Hit of it all . . . ' belle of the ball . . . hope I don't fall . . . ."

"It's time to go, I think."

"Oh, I'm back to form now, Elaine, thanks to you."

"What have I done?" Elaine moaned as they walked back outside. She tweaked Sheila's braid. "Why don't you take the plunge and have your hair cut and styled? You'd be a knockout."

"Who wants to be a knockout? If I knocked people out, I wouldn't have anyone to listen to my corny poems."

Elaine shook her head, laughing as she walked with Sheila to her car. "You are incredible, you know. You have so much, and yet you're so . . . oh, I don't know . . . *humble* about it, I guess. I wish I had a dose of whatever it is, though."

Sheila shot her an amazed look. "I don't have anything you don't have, except—" she smiled slowly, her eyes twinkling again—my faith. That's really what keeps me up, you know, and you can have the same thing if you want it."

Elaine laughed. "Okay, okay. I've listened to that line for five years now. Maybe eventually it will crack even a hard nut like me."

Sheila tossed the parcels containing new dress, shoes, purse, lingerie into the back seat, then slid in behind the wheel and shut the door. "Beware the hard-shell nut," she pronounced with solemn finality. "You'll end up a nut in a rut with every door shut." Then she started the car, waved merrily. "Thanks for all the help. I'll call and tell you all about it if I live through it." The irony of those last laughing words would not strike her until much, much later.

Friday night the Choir Foibles and Follies was performed without a hitch. Saturday, Sheila indulged in a rare late morning, basking in the memories of the jubilant cast and standing ovation of the audience. After lunch she realized she had forgotten to have the gas and oil in her yellow Capri checked before driving to Roanoke. By the time she had run by the service station, studied her Sunday school lesson and washed her hair, which took eons because of its extraordinary length, it was too late to do more than inhale a sandwich. She wheeled into the airport parking lot and dashed inside just in time to fling her poems at Daniel, who had been pacing the floor and eyeing his watch with growing agitation.

At twenty minutes before nine Sheila screeched back into her driveway. After what had to be the fastest shower and change of clothes in history, she stood before the dresser mirror for one agonizing moment, deliberating over her hair. Maybe Elaine had been right, after all. With nose-wrinkling shrug, she decided to literally let it all hang, so after unbraiding the mass and brushing through it enough to remove the tangles, she stuck one of her mother's tortoise shell combs over one ear and left with only a backward glance at the reflection in the mirror.

The dress was a cut above the average, she decided, an off-the-shoulder style in a deep, shimmering royal blue polyester as soft and whispery fine as silk. She and Elaine had laughingly decided that when Sheila made her first million, she'd definitely settle for nothing but silk, but for now . . . .

. . . . For now she was on top of the world. Daniel had been enthusiastic after his brief glimpse of her cards; she was going to make it to the party on time; *and* she was going to be . . . herself. "Or at least as much of myself as Doris can stand," she grinned, then chuckled as she imagined Doris' expression if she committed some hilarious *faux pas* upon meeting the infamous Cole Hampton.

Joe and Doris were standing by a massive stone fireplace when Sheila arrived and she waved to them after the uniformed butler let her in through the huge double doors gracing the front entrance of the stylish California mission style estate.

"I'm so glad you're here." Doris gripped her hand hard as Joe kissed her cheek and winked. "Thanks for coming. Did you see Daniel all right? Did you have any trouble getting here?"

"You're welcome, yes, and no." Sheila grinned indulgently at her friend. "It doesn't look that bad, Doris . . . ." Her eyes wandered over the crowd of people, and she gave an inward shudder before admonishing herself sternly. In a deliberately bright voice she asked, "How many people are here, anyway?"

"The party is open to all Mr. Hampton's employees, their guests, and all the local officials and dignitaries," Joe told her. "So between now and whenever, there could be as many as two hundred at any one time."

"And all of them having a good time but me," Doris wailed.

"Nonsense," Sheila retorted. She looked around some more. "Well, it doesn't exactly look like a lion's den, but I'm ready if you are. Come on—you got me here, so you might as well give in and enjoy it as I plan to."

Within ten minutes two of Joe's officemates had come over to be introduced, and within twenty minutes their particular corner had mushroomed into a lively group bandying about a cheerful conversation on a variety of topics. Frequent bursts of laughter attested to the success of Sheila's offbeat sense of humor, but if anyone had mentioned to her that she was the hub of this phenomenal development, she would have denied it. She enjoyed talking with people, after all, and of course people enjoyed talking back. It was truly amazing that after all her apprehension about the evening, she had discovered this was really not so intimidating after all.

A man standing across the room talking to a bored looking but beautiful woman eventually noticed the group. There were cliques and groups of people all over his rambling home, and the bulk of them were carrying on a conversation, albeit loud and laced with liquor. But there was some sort of electricity pulsating from that particular collection of individuals by his fireplace.

The man narrowed his gaze, assessing what it was about them that was making them so obvious. When it hit him, he felt as if a fist had just been jammed into his stomach. They looked—*happy*. Relaxed, interested, as if they were really enjoying themselves. The rest of his employees and guests all appeared to have been mass-produced as dolls to whom all expression was forbidden, unless, of course, they happened to be talking to *him*. Then they managed a sort of servile attentiveness that irritated him to the point of insanity.

Cole Hampton was not overly fond of his fellow man, and at times he made no attempt to hide it. He hated throwing these annual bashes, but knew from years of experience that people worked better if they also had a chance to relax together. Though how anyone could possibly term this melee 'relaxing' was beyond him. The steady drone of inane conversation, the choking cigarette smoke and fumes of alcohol . . . the blend of perfume and after-shave was offensive. In fact, if he weren't the host, he'd walk out and never look back. But these people depended on him, looked up to him, God help him, and he knew there was no way out. The woman who had been talking to him now put her hand on his arm, stroking it with her long, painted nails and smiling up at him through a screen of false eyelashes. He abruptly freed himself with an undoubtedly brusque remark and began maneuvering his way toward the group by the fireplace.

He was stopped frequently, and his cold gray eyes grew colder, the color of granite and just as giving. After Jay Stetson, one of his accountants, asked him for the third time that week about his addition of two more computers, he snapped out a barely civil reply.

Stetson scuttled off with a resigned but knowing smile on his face. Cole knew the word would now spread rapidly that he was in one of his black 'moods.'

Ah, what the—suddenly, his eye was arrested by the face of a young woman. She was laughing, not a falsely condescending laugh nor obnoxious guffaw, but a sweetly lilting laugh that was audible even where he stood. Her face was smooth, free of make-up except for the lightest dusting of blusher on her cheeks. And her eyes . . . they were huge, like a startled doe, and alight with a kind of merriment that he had seen only in the faces of very young children. When she turned to speak to a man beside her, her hair swirled and rippled like a wave of shimmering brown silk cloth. It spilled about her shoulders and fell almost to her waist, and he wanted to bury his face in it with an urge that was so sharp, so poignant, that it was almost physical. As if in a daze he moved toward her, recognizing on some very elemental level that she was the reason all those people looked so very much alive. He had to meet her, had to find out if she was real or some mirage, some trick his world-weary brain had conjured up to help him through the evening.

"Joe." He nodded to his new Vice-President for Research, and smiled at Doris. Then his eyes moved to Sheila, who had turned to him with a smile that took his breath away. "Introduce me to this lovely young woman."

"Cole," Joe nodded to his boss genially, taking Sheila's arm through his own, "this is Sheila Jamison. Sheila, Cole Hampton, my boss and the host of this affair."

Sheila's eyes widened, and she was unable to hide her startled reaction. She hadn't actually expected to meet him, and she definitely had not expected him to look like—like this. He was almost brutally masculine, with an aura of tightly leashed tension that made

23

her think of a rippling-muscled panther waiting to pounce, with his tail lashing slowly and ominously back and forth. About six feet tall, he towered over her own five feet four even with her flimsy evening sandals, and there didn't appear to be an ounce of spare flesh on the powerful body. He was all hard bone and steely muscles from the arrogant blade of his slashing nose to the toes of his undoubtedly custom-made shoes. Right now he was looking at her as if he'd like to have her for dinner, and the smoldering desire of that look almost served to throw her completely off balance. She held out her hand with a strange reluctance, and when his engulfed it, holding it in a firm grip that could have smashed every bone if he chose, she felt as if she had just stuck it inside the module of a power generator.

"Hi," she managed, her tongue as well as her brain temporarily short-circuited. What had happened to the bottomless well of conversation?

Cole stared down directly into her face, his razor-sharp eyes not missing her response. He smiled, a slow, predatory smile that sent two creases knifing down the lean planes of his cheeks.

"Hello," he replied, knowing amusement in the two syllables that caused a band of color to stain across her cheeks.

Sheila tried to tug her hand free discreetly and for a moment almost panicked until he let it go. She glanced around, catching Doris' eye with frantic appeal in her gaze.

"Sheila is a very dear friend," Doris jumped in headfirst, almost gushing the words. "I asked her to come tonight because I—" She came skidding to a halt as she realized what she had been about to reveal, and Sheila felt her anguished consternation as if it were her own.

With reckless disregard for consequences Sheila turned to Cole, the light of battle in her eyes. If he dared say anything . . . .

"—Because I bullied her until she gave in. I've never been in this part of town, or invited to your renowned open house, and the chance was too good to miss. I need the first-hand experience, you see, to document the dissertation I'm writing on contemporary lifestyles of the rich, very-rich, and too-disgusting-for-words-rich. Doris was afraid I might write something controversial about you and you'd fire Joe for revenge. Or demote him to pasting labels in the stock room. Will you?"

It was as if there was nobody else in the room. All the other people seemed to disappear into the wrong end of a telescope as Sheila stared up into the face of a man the likes of whom she had never met in all her twenty-four years. She was absolutely numb with mortification, caught by her personality quirks like a worm writing on a hook. There were any number of things she could have said—or even done—that would have kept her poise and Doris's from crumbling into dust. What on earth had possessed her to spin such a dreadful tale? She could think of at least twenty verses off the top of her head where the Bible expressly forbade lying, and here she was lying with the artfulness of old Scratch himself.

"No, I wouldn't."

"Wh—what?" there was amusement on his face now; the slate gray eyes were warm with it and his mouth, so firm and set, was twitching suspiciously. Sheila stared up at him.

"I wouldn't fire him or demote him," Cole repeated patiently. His eyebrow arched as the gray eyes seemed to pour over her like melted silver. "Are you really writing a doctoral dissertation?"

"No. I'm sorry—I shouldn't have—"

"Don't apologize. Actually it ought to make for interesting reading if you do ever decide to do one." He stepped toward her, subtly but definitely edging Joe out of the way so that he and Sheila were side by side. "Just to satisfy my curiosity . . . if you *were* writing a dissertation, into which category would I fall?"

Sheila gaped at him, and then blushed like a schoolgirl. If she ever made it out of here in one piece she would never, *ever*, pull that particular stunt again. She would, perhaps, even move to Bangor, Maine to avoid the remote possibility of ever running into him accidentally . . . .

She was saved the embarrassment of trying to come up with an answer, however. An older woman who looked like a housekeeper had come up and was reluctantly making a bid for Cole Hampton's attention by tapping him on the arm. He couldn't ignore it and turned. Sheila shuddered, and hoped that nobody would ever give her the kind of look the hapless woman was receiving now.

"What is it, Ada?" His voice was polite, but barely.

"You have a phone call, Mr. Hampton. It's Mr. Minkowitz, or I never would have disturbed you." she cast a vaguely apologetic look around as if to appease not only her employer but those of his guests whose expression ranged from merely curious to alarmed.

"All right, Ada. I'm on my way." He ignored the others, but looked back at Sheila with a brief, all-encompassing glance that caused a fresh flow of color to surge through her cheeks. Then he was gone, without apology or explanation, and it was as if the mountain lion had just left the chicken coop. There was an audible collective sigh, with relief and speculation washing over the group like ripples in a pool.

"I hope it's not too serious," someone commented, and there were murmurs of assent and anxiety.

"What is it?" Doris asked, and Joe took her hand reassuringly.

"Apparently there's a problem of some kind at the

plant. It could be serious, since Herb's not the kind of guy to get rattled easily and call Cole away from the middle of a party."

"Oh, dear." Doris reached with her free hand and held it momentarily against her husband's cheek. "I'm sure he'll work it out, honey. Try not to worry."

Everyone made an effort to resume normal conversation, and though Sheila was still unnerved by her introduction and subsequent behavior with the head of Hampton Electronics, she doubled her efforts to keep the party from falling flat. She felt a strange obligation not to let Cole Hampton down, which in itself was unsettling when she had made such an appalling idiot of herself. Things seemed to settle down after awhile even though everyone knew Cole had driven out to the plant. After an hour and a half, Sheila decided it was time to go home. It was going on midnight, and tomorrow was church, after all. Hopefully she had managed to erase the earlier behavior from everyone's memory. She excused herself from the group of three men who had been heatedly but genially debating with her about the relevance of past history to current events. After making her way to Doris and Joe and telling them goodnight—and reassuring them that she didn't mind driving alone— she slipped outside into the summer night.

Darkness and solitude enfolded her like a soft velvet blanket, and she breathed the fresh scents thankfully. Rolling down the window in her car, she drove slowly along the long winding gravel drive, savoring the softness of the breeze and the far off chirrup of crickets calling out a love song.

Cole Hampton had bought fifty acres of prime woodland as the setting for his home; Sheila was grateful that he had cleared only enough for the house and three miles of driveway. The rest had been left as nature created it, and she knew in the daytime it would be breathtaking. It was pitch-black now, but

Sheila didn't mind, for it was actually a welcome change from the past several hours. Only now did she admit how tense she was, and how tired. It would be a blessed relief to fall into bed tonight, and she mouthed a little prayer of thankfulness that the evening was over. *And oh, yes, Lord,* she added, feeling heat stealing over her cheeks even now, *forgive me for the way I acted with Cole.* She closed her eyes briefly, a fraction of a second, and when she opened them it was to see two blinding headlights hurtling at her with what seemed to be impossible speed.

CHAPTER 2

"THE MAIL JUST CAME. HANNAH." Sheila called to a large, comfortably plump woman. "I'm going to get it and then walk around the yard."

"Don't stray too far afield." The older woman watched as Sheila wandered slowly down the porch steps and across the grass to the mailbox. Compassion swam in her faded blue eyes which were surrounded by hundreds of criss-cross lines that had deepened over the last six months. There had been so little change, even some deterioration in the too-slender young woman who had hired her to be watchdog as well as housekeeper.

Sheila leafed through the several envelopes and circulars with little interest, though a brief spark flickered in dull brown eyes as she noted a postcard from the Allendre's. They were spending two weeks in the Carribean, and wished Sheila were there to see how beautiful everything was. "See . . . ." Sheila sighed, and her hand lifted from habit to rub over her eyes and forehead. The scar that marred her forehead and left temple had faded now to a thin white line, but the damage inside hadn't changed. She wondered, as she did every breathing moment and even in her restless dreams, when the next episode would occur. It had been two weeks now, so any moment she could expect it. As she meandered aimlessly around the yard she tried to appreciate the freshness, the loveliness of spring in full bloom. The foresythias were a riotous yellow, and the dogwood in the corner was redolent with pink-white blossoms. The daisies her mother had planted with such loving hands were starting to flourish as well, although there were no longer any hands that tended them beyond the watering and occasional weeding Hannah gave them.

The fear and uncertainty that had become a part of her welled up inside, turning the sunshiny April day to a colorless, clammy gray cloak of fog. With a tremulous sigh she turned back to the house. She handed Hannah the mail as she sat down at the kitchen table, running nervous fingers through the careless mop of short curls. "We got a card from Joe and Doris," she commented.

"So I see," Hannah scanned the scrawled lines and put it down. "I'm glad they're having a good time. The good Lord knows they deserve it."

"Doris told me it's the first vacation they've had alone in twenty years. It was nice of Cole Hampton to let Joe have the time."

Hannah glanced at her sharply, but there was nothing in her voice but matter-of-fact, casual interest. But then, everyone had conspired to make sure it stayed that way. Still . . . she couldn't help but wonder sometimes. "Hmm? What'd you say, love?"

"I said I've been doing some thinking." Her fingers ran through the soft mass of curls again, finally eliciting Hannah's full attention. Sheila always did that when she was particularly nervous, as well as a few other habits that Hannah was forever pointing out to her in the kindest of ways. She sighed. 'I'll never get used to it like this, but I suppose under the circumstances it ought to stay."

"I've told you for—let's see—five months and about two weeks now that if you want to let it grow back out I would be more than happy to help you take care of it."

"You do too much as it is," Sheila all but snapped. There was a moment of strained silence before she wearily lifted her hand in a gesture of apology. "I'm sorry. No one could possibly be as helpful and understanding as you, Hannah. But that's what I've been thinking about. You're *so* helpful that I'm finding myself depending on you more and more, and you know as well as I do that that's not right. Someday I'm going to have to learn how to cope on my own— you can't stay with me forever." She looked down at the worn maple table, tracing her finger along one of the many cracks. "And the way it's going, I'm not going to be able to afford you much longer."

Hannah settled into the chair next to her and wrapped a motherly arm about her shoulder. "Now you just hush all that talk. I'll be here as long as you need me, regardless of whether you pay me or not." She squeezed Sheila's rigid shoulders. "Are you trying to insult me or something? I've got George's social security, and you know the church—"

"I know, I know." She moved restlessly, but Hannah refused to move her arm. "I *know* we'll both be taken care of, and I *know* it's all being done out of love and not pity. But, Hannah, I haven't been able to write anything decent in three months now. I do feel some obligation to pay my bills."

"If you'd go back to your inspirational poems instead of all this other stuff, I bet you'd find the money problems vanishing—or at least less of a burden."

"I can't." There was a poignant pause. "I seem to have lost all my inspiration nine months ago, and I can't find it." She stood up, moved to the sink, and stared out the window. "sometimes I wish I'd just be permanently blind instead of this—never knowing from day to day. At least then I could get a cane and be done with it."

"Sheila Jamison, I ought to put you across my knee! You should be thanking God for the moments you are able to see instead of always worrying about the moments you can't." Her normally amiable voice was stern, and she glared at Sheila's back like a teacher brandishing a hickory stick.

Sheila turned around, the ghost of a smile on her face. "I know," she responded quietly.

The sunlight streaming through the window reflected almost cruelly the changes in her over the last nine months. Her once long hair had had to be cropped after the crash, a portion even shaved after they found out about her sight.

Elaine had been a true friend then. She had hauled Sheila off to the beauty parlor and made her get a permanent, then raved enthusiastically about the result. But Sheila knew she had lost more than her hair, and so did everyone else. Her dancing brown eyes, once so full of laughter and life, were still as large, still framed by impossibly dark lashes. The light had gone out of them, however, and they didn't dance anymore. Her expression was always a little bit sad, a little bit haunted, a little bit fearful. The doctors had been sympathetic—and saddened. They told her that there was a miniscule piece of metal embedded in her brain in such a manner as to be virtually inoperable. Worse yet, it was not stationary and anything—twisting her head, bending over—could cause it to shift and pinch the optic nerve, thus causing total blindness for an indefinite period. The shortest, thus far, had been six hours; the longest, three days. And one day it might be permanent.

Nobody had known the first day that her sight had

been affected. She had just been thankful to be alive and—she thought—relatively undamaged save the myriad cuts, bruises, and abrasions. The man driving the other car had fared a lot worse, breaking an arm and collarbone and suffering a concussion. But he, too, would be fine and Sheila considered it a minor miracle. The police had asked if she wanted to press charges, but after finding out that he had been swerving to miss a couple from the party out for a late stroll, she had refused.

"He was trying to avoid a worse tragedy," she had stated with unequivocal firmness to the astonished policeman. "He wasn't drunk, or even speeding, and I will not burden him or make him pay for trying to save peoples' lives." She had never even found out who it was, for it was right after that the blindness struck. Then she didn't care about anything but fighting the fear, the depression, the rapid withdrawal into a state of shock that had taken months to dissipate.

Evie Meadows from church had found Hannah for her. Hannah was Evie's aunt, and since her husband had died the year before, she had been lonely and restless. Coming to live with Sheila had been good for both of them, though it was a long time before Sheila felt comfortable enough to ask for help when she needed it.

It was ultimately Hannah who kept her from sinking into an abyss of total depression, where even her faith had not followed. Hannah treated her with a matter-of-fact motherliness when she was blind, and as an endearing but wayward child when she could see. She bullied her into eating, she cajoled her into taking long walks, she shamed her into at least reading her Bible again, although the verses seemed to slide off her heart like water off a duck's back. But Hannah didn't berate her when she quit teaching her fifth grade Sunday school class, or admonish her for turning to

33

purely secular greeting cards as her source of income. It was as if she knew that Sheila was in a spiritual wilderness, and that she would have to do her own wandering before she returned. Sheila had never felt any bitterness, for she knew enough to understand that God had not caused the accident, nor was she being punished. She had never had her faith tested like this before, however, and she had a lot of doubts, a lot of questions. Even the death of her parents had not produced the trauma to her faith, because even then Sheila had accepted that they were with God and she would see them again someday. But this . . . this was something that wasn't cut and dried, like a wound that just needed time to heal completely. She was festering inside with a malignancy that was only hurting more with time, and she didn't know how to handle it.

"I want to get away," she stated now, flatly. "I want to go somewhere where I'm completely on my own, where there is nobody to depend on but myself." She held up her hand to keep Hannah from interrupting. "Hannah, please try to understand. I've lost my freedom to drive a car; I've lost most of the creativity that God gave me; I've lost all the joy, my faith . . . . I feel like I've at least got to make a stab at finding my self-respect and independence. I've had almost eight months now to learn how to cope when I'm blind—I can dress, wash, even boil water and fix myself a sandwich without making a mess. It's time for me to let go of you and prove to myself that I can go it alone—if I ever *have* to."

"But, Sheila—"

"Dear, Hannah, I love you, but even *you* aren't indestructible. You could have a heart attack, or your grandchildren could need you or anyone of a number of other things. If I've learned nothing else these past months, I've learned that nothing in life is certain." She stared the housekeeper down, and for the first time in many months there was a hint of color in her cheeks. "Elaine's parents have a cabin on a lake out of Roanoke. She said I could use it—they won't be going up there until June." Her voice dropped, and her hands twisted together in unconscious supplication. "Will you drive me up there, Hannah? Please?"

There was a long period of silence, and she found herself noting crazy irrelevant details, like the place in the shiny linoleum that dipped from the foundation settling . . . the crisp white priscillas softly billowing from the gentle spring breeze and tugging gently on the peperomia Hannah had brought from her own home . . . the smell of fresh white-acre peas they had just put on to boil for supper . . . .

"All right, honey, I'll take you." Hannah's voice was reluctant but resigned, and Sheila's heart started thumping again in slow, hurtful throbs. "When do you want to leave?"

"As soon as possible. It won't take long to pack, since I'll only be carrying jeans and things. I thought I'd try it for a week, and if it's going okay or if I don't have a spell, then I'll just stay on awhile longer. I'm taking the stuff I'm working on—it isn't due until May first, but I'll need something to do." She knew she was talking too fast but it was as if a tiny trickle had just burst into a geyser. The need to get away had been rumbling away in the background, and now that it was out in the open, she could hardly wait. Anything was better than her present lifestyle.

The cabin was a quiet jewel set among a stand of pines. The deciduous hardwoods were starting to green out and pockets of purple curlflowers and dainty white Rue Anemone—and others Sheila didn't recognize in spite of years of exposure to her mother's love of flowers—had been flung with a lavish hand about the clearing. Even the stubbornly quiet Hannah was charmed. The cabin itself was spartan, but squeaky

35

clean, and there were no stairs to fall down. Sheila couldn't help but toss an I-told-you-so look over her shoulder as they explored the premises.

"And the lake is a good hundred yards away, so you needn't worry that I'll fall in," she added for good measure.

They rummaged around the kitchen, and Hannah satisfied herself that the range and oven were modern and easy enough for even a blind person to use.

"Here's the phone," Sheila called from the bedroom. There was only one with a charming cherry four-poster bed covered by a quilt in a wedding ring pattern. She picked up the phone and held the receiver to her ear. "And it works, just like Elaine promised!"

She walked out into the main living room, surveying the spare but comfortable furnishings with a blend of excitement and fear. She made sure she kept the fear well hidden from Hannah. "The fireplace is nice," she called again, running her hand over the rough bricks and then the huge oak beam that served as the mantel. "I doubt I'll have much use for it, though."

"I should think not," Hannah snorted as she joined Sheila, her large body moving ponderously across the large braided rug that covered the floor. "My mind refuses to contemplate all the things that could happen if you—"

"Hannah, if you say one more word about the things that could happen to me up here all by myself, I'll—I'll fire you!" Sheila smiled to soften the words, to let Hannah know she was only teasing, but her voice was a shade high, a shade uncertain. "I have promised to call faithfully every night between nine and ten o'clock, and to let you know immediately if I need help. Elaine says there are a couple of other homes on the other side of the lake, and in an emergency I can always call over there."

"You don't know who they belong to, much less if there is someone there right now."

Sheila took a deep, steadying breath. "I'm not going to discuss it anymore. I'm staying, and I'm staying alone. You better start back if you want to make it before it starts getting dark. "I'll call you in about three hours."

She stayed outside on the porch after Hannah left, rocking in one of the huge Brumby rockers and letting all the tension dribble out like sand through an hourglass. Yes, she was afraid. God Himself knew jut how afraid she really was, but then He probably also knew how desperate she had been to take this step. She stayed out there, rocking slowly and watching the shadows gradually lengthen, and wished that she could find some of the peace that this little cabin had stored in its walls.

She slept little, and only nibbled at her supper, a delicious beef stew Hannah had left. Lying beneath the covers of the surprisingly firm bed, she wondered when it would happen. She wondered how she would react when it did, and what she would be doing. There was never any warning. One minute she would be performing some mundane task as painless as dusting the furniture, and the next thing she knew, the world was black as pitch. She wondered if she would do something disgracefully humiliating like bursting into hysterical sobs. She never had, not even the first time when the fear had clawed up her throat and tried to choke her. No . . . she had never cried. Christians were supposed to endure cheerfully, and she had already let God down more than once. The least she could do was to maintain a stoic front before the world. She fell asleep at last, listening to the haunting call of a whip poor will, and the tears burned slowly, unknowingly down her cheeks as she slept.

It was almost noon before she ventured outside. The sun was shining in a cloudless sky, and a playful breeze whispered enticingly through the pines. Rich earthy smells—of water and humous and pinestraw and pungent sap—tugged at her senses until she gave in. She would count the steps down the path to the lake, and remember which side of her face the sun was shining on, so that if the blindness came, she would be able to make it back to the cabin.

But the water was gleaming, winking like a shimmering mirror through the trees, and Sheila found her footsteps following the path until the cabin was quite out of sight. It was so quiet, so clean out here, and she felt sort of a tentative calm welling up in her and gradually subduing the quavering fear. She decided to just follow the path willy-nilly to see where it went and hope that she would retain her vision. Besides, just a little way beyond, she saw some flowering plants that she thought might be the lovely Lady's Slipper, and she wanted to investigate. Hazy notions of writing down all the varieties of wildflowers found here were taking shape in her brain when she rounded a bend and all but collided with a man.

His back had been to her, but at her sharply indrawn gasp, he whipped about and they stared at each other like wary animals. She saw a tallish man who looked to be in his middle thirties, with a shock of unruly black hair streaked at the temples with glittering silver strands. His eyes were as gray as the lake, but about as welcoming as a storm cloud. Somewhere in the farthest recesses of her brain something clicked, and a queer sense of *deja vu* tingled down her spine. Had she met him before?

"If you're following me, I feel I better warn you that I'd as soon toss you in the lake as to give you the time of day." His voice was as friendly as a thundercloud, too, and Sheila backed a step.

"I wasn't following you," she informed him in bewilderment. "I'm staying in the cabin—" she waved her arm uncertainly in the direction of the cabin, "—back there, and just came for a walk."

The man was staring at her now, with an intentness that would have been insulting if it hadn't been so intimidating. "Do I know you?" he suddenly ground out, his deep voice irritated as if he hated to voice the trite question.

"No!" blurted Sheila, too quickly, and the man's eyes narrowed to slits. He took a step toward her and, with a haste that later would cause her to blush with humiliation, she turned and ran back down the path toward the cabin.

Hours later, as she sat at the kitchen table with a mug of coffee between her hands, she alternately berated herself for the stupidity of her reaction and then searched corners of her brain trying to remember where she might have seen the man before. He had been so hostile that she dreaded another encounter, yet she had to face that possibility unless she intended to spend the entire week cooped up in the cabin like a timid mouse.

She spent another restless night, and upon waking with the dawn decided to take her walk now with the hope that the man would not be up this early. He had looked to be the type who spent all night partying and then slept until noon. She paused in the process of pulling on her jeans. What on earth made her conjure up a description like that? He was more probably a loner, someone who had come up here for the same reason she had—to be alone—and he probably had been up fishing for at least an hour. Shaking her head in irritation, she finished dressing and then started across the room. At that moment her vision was snuffed out with the swiftness of a guillotine.

She was relieved that her immediate reaction was— relief. It had finally happened and the waiting was over. Now was the time of real testing, when there was no Hannah to call, no willing friends to fill the frightening void with cheerful chatter and reassuring pats. Breakfast. She needed to eat something and now was as good a time as any to try out her skill in the kitchen. Alone. As she slowly, cautiously, step by hesitant step, felt her way to the kitchen, vivid pictures tumbled over themselves in her memory . . . . Hannah, hovering anxiously at her shoulder the first time she heated a can of soup, hugging her in relief when she only spilled a few drops . . . laughing a booming laugh and prodding her to join in when in attempting to scramble eggs, Sheila poured them all over the stove instead of in the frying pan . . . . Doris, suggesting that she "practice" by using a blindfold, and then blindfolding herself so she could understand . . . .

Sheila's forehead and temples were damp, hands trembling, when at last she felt for and found the ladderback chair next to the kitchen table. Breathing in deep, shuddering gasps, she sat there for a few minutes, fighting to remain calm and not fumble for the telephone like a whimpering baby, afraid of the dark. Maybe if she prayed, she'd feel better. She tried, but the words seemed to fall into a bottomless void, and there seemed to be no one to hear—no one to answer. She knew it was her own fault, that fear and doubt and apathy had erected the barrier. God had not turned His back; she had turned hers.

After awhile she stood, stiffening her resolve and her backbone—and just as abruptly as it had left, her sight was restored. She blinked, gazing around in a daze as her mind attempted to adjust to this rapid reversal of circumstances. It had only lasted about twenty minutes this time—was that good, or bad? Should she call home? The answer to that last question was a resounding *no:* she knew as surely as she was sitting here that Hannah would be on her like a duck on a June bug. With grim resolve, she made herself breakfast and then walked outside to enjoy the spring morning.

Two days passed, with her evening phone call to Hannah carefully concealing the doubts and fears that continued to plague her. She had gone for several more walks, but had not seen the man again, and was bewildered to discover that a part of her was almost disappointed. She wrote verses for two birthday cards and a promotion congratulations, read old copies of *Reader's Digest* and *National Geographic*, skimped on meals and continued to look like an insubstantial wraith fading away into nothing.

The fourth day she met him again. She had gone for her usual sunset stroll when he appeared from the opposite direction, jogging at an easy clip and wearing a ragged pair of jogging shorts and beat-up Nikes. The dark curling hairs that matted his body were damp with sweat, and the muscles of his arms and chest glistened as if they had been oiled. He was overwhelmingly male and Sheila couldn't help the gaping stare that told him so. He stopped in front of her, mockery glinting in the gray eyes as his breath escaped in panting little puffs.

"I wondered if I'd scared you off for good—you took off like a rabbit with a pack of hounds at its heels the other day."

Sheila flushed, but stood her ground. "I admit I was a little frightened, but that's because you caught me off guard. I came up here to enjoy the solitude and not even a rude, overbearing man is going to drive me away."

"Well, I came up here for some solitude, also, and no scruffy little girl with a mop of hair and big brown eyes is going to deprive me of it." he grinned as the color bloomed hectically all over her face and neck. "I've never met a woman who blushes—" He stopped abruptly, all the color draining from his face as his eyes darkened to charcoal. "Oh, no!" he moaned hoarsely, and the hands hanging loosely at his sides tightened into white-knuckled fists. "It can't be . . . ."

41

"What's the matter?" Sheila whispered, feeling almost overwhelmed by the raw emotion she was witnessing.

"What's your name?" he ground the words, spitting them out like crushed glass. Then, as he seemed to realize he was frightening her, the expression on his face softened fractionally. "Please," he added, and this time his voice, though still hard as steel, held a thread of supplication that Sheila couldn't ignore.

"Sheila Jamison." She jerked as his hand came up toward her face, but he only fingered the shorn wisps of hair, and something like a wince flickered behind the now-shuttered eyes.

"Ah . . . ." The breath expelled from him in a sigh that was almost a groan. Then, with a gentleness that held her spellbound, frozen in place, his hand traced a path along the line of her jaw, across to her heated cheek, and discovered the faint but definite ridge of the scar. "We have met before, Sheila Jamison, but it's all too obvious that you don't remember." He hesitated, then smiled a twisted smile that stabbed at her heart. "I'm Cole Hampton. We met last year at my open house." He was watching her closely, the gray eyes moving restlessly over each feature of her face and cataloging every nuance of emotion.

Sheila was too stunned to notice. "Cole Hampton?" she repeated. "Joe's boss—Hampton Electronics?"

"The same. Do you remember now?"

His voice was curt, and Sheila wondered is she had offended him. "Yes," she replied in a low voice. "I remember. I—I just didn't expect to see you up here—I never really expected to see you again."

She couldn't look at him, because superimposing the horrors of that tragic night was the memory of her introduction to Cole. She had made a prize idiot of herself, and if he hadn't been called away, she would have died of shame. She smiled a little, trying to lighten the deepening currents that were threatening to engulf her. "I made a fool of myself, as I recall. Then you had to leave." She looked up at him at last, and almost recoiled at the look on his face. "I'm sorry if I've offended you by not recognizing you. You see, maybe you didn't know since you had to leave that night after we met that I—" She hesitated, then finished in a colorless tone—"that I had an accident while I was driving home. I'm afraid that memory has overshadowed everything else."

"I know." That frightening look of grim implacability had faded somewhat, and he studied her now as if trying to decide what to say next. "You don't have to apologize."

"I'll be leaving then," she offered, thinking that he probably wanted to escape the awkward situation and was afraid of hurting her feelings. "You said you came here to be alone, and I did, too. I promise to try and stay out of your way from now on and . . . ."

"Why did you cut your hair?"

She gaped at him, her hand rising involuntarily to her shorn head. "I—uh, I had to after the accident . . . ."

"Let it grow," he said, and then turned and ran as if he couldn't bear to be around her any longer.

Sheila stood there for long minutes, fighting an absurd desire to cry. Her memories of Cole Hampton were not all exactly pleasant, but she couldn't forget him, couldn't shake the fascination he had engendered in her during that brief five minutes so long ago. He had been the most compelling, the most intriguing man she had ever met, and though she knew that she would probably never see him again, her heart still quickened at the mention of his name. And now she *had* met him again, and he had been abrupt, almost rude, unpleasant and unsettling. But her face still tingled from the brush of those strong but infinitely tender fingers. *I wish I knew what to think*, she pondered as at last she made her way back to the cabin. *I wish I could talk to the Lord like I used to and know that I would get an answer. And more than anything else . . . I wish Cole Hampton liked me.*

He continued to run until his lungs were bursting and his vision blurred, but nothing could erase the burning memories of that August night nine months ago. She looked so fragile, so pale and unhappy now. And her glorious hair! What had he done? And what would Sheila Jamison's reaction be if he told her why he knew all about her accident? If he told her that he was the man who had been driving the other car!

Was he also responsible for transforming her from the most vibrant woman he had ever met to this empty, lifeless shell? Renewed guilt washed over him like acid, eating him from the inside out until he wanted to scream out the agony. He had started many times in those first weeks to go to her and apologize, but at the last minute had always dredged up an excuse. He couldn't face the shock of recognition, the accusations, the recriminations he knew he deserved.

When his lawyer told him she wasn't going to press charges, Cole couldn't believe it, because she could have made a justifiably large settlement. He had felt guiltier than ever, especially when, after pressing Joe Allendre, he was told that Sheila thought he was so noble for trying to save those idiots' lives. But why had it had to be Sheila? He had been determined, after that fascinating introduction, to charm her into at least an affair, but after his own injuries had healed, he had found himself reluctant to pursue the matter. Joe had been curiously evasive the time or two he casually mentioned her name, and after a couple of months, he had just shrugged aside the whole matter. It was over, and the girl apparently hadn't been seriously injured. He had become immersed in business—and other women—and had actually forgotten about Sheila Jamison. Until today.

He knew he would have recognized her after the first amusing encounter the other day if she hadn't cut her hair, even though she had lost weight and her extraordinary eyes weren't filled with light. At the time he had laughed as she scampered off so wildly, thinking of how easily he had managed to send some impressionable but unwanted female off, with her tail between her legs. Well, he wasn't laughing now, and in fact felt as if hot ground glass was churning up his insides.

Her hair had been so beautiful, as bright and shining as the woman herself, and because of that blasted accident she had cut it off. And what was she doing up here—apparently alone—looking as if she were three-quarters dead? It couldn't have anything to do with the accident—she had sustained only surface injuries, he was told, and would have healed months ago. So what was she doing here?

He was almost as angry with Sheila as he was with himself, especially when he had to admit that he was no more able to ignore her now than he could ignore a computer whose read-out sheet had malfunctioned. He and Ms. Sheila Jamison were going to have an accounting—and then she could hibernate in her blasted cabin for all he cared. He had come up here on his first vacation in three years and no woman, however piquant and tragic, was going to spoil it.

He walked back toward his own lakeside retreat with determined vigor, allowing his body to cool down as well as his temper. After he showered and changed clothes, he might just take a notion to drop in on her unexpectedly, knowing from vast experience that women were more vulnerable when kept off balance. It was almost ridiculously easy to throw this one off balance, anyway, and the prospect of provoking that delightful blush had him whistling as he took the stairs leading to the back door, two at a time.

CHAPTER 3

WHEN THE KNOCK CAME Sheila was so startled she dropped the pen she was holding. Her heart started pounding and ice-cold needles seemed to be pricking her skin. She knew of only one person it could possibly be.

"Can I come in?" he asked with deceptive softness when she opened the door.

"If you like." Innate manners dictated her answer even as her brain clanged all sorts of warning bells. "Was there something you wanted . . . or needed to ask me about?" She found herself retreating as he sauntered through the door, acting for all the world like the Oates' tomcat, prowling around new territory, preparing to stake a claim. The thought was suddenly not at all amusing. She was all alone, and he outweighed her by at least a hundred pounds.

"Stop looking as if I'm going to attack you," he murmured lazily, wandering over to the cardboard table she had set up in front of the fireplace. "What are you doing, anyway?"

"Working. I write all those cute little verses you

read inside greeting cards." Her answer had come out a little more bluntly than she had intended, and she took note of Cole's lifted eyebrow in response.

"Why the sarcasm? Don't you enjoy what you do?"

The careless words stabbed deeply, and Sheila felt the blood draining from her face. "Not any more," she muttered, turning from him abruptly and staring blindly out the large picture window that faced the lake.

Cole moved to stand directly behind her, noting the rigidity of the slender shoulders, the way her hands were tightly hugging her waist. "What are you doing up here all by yourself, Sheila Jamison?" His hand reached and grasped her chin, turning her face to his penetrating gaze. "Are you trying to get over a sour love affair?"

"No!" Sheila gasped, wrenching free and staring up at him in horror. "What a terrible thing to suggest! Do you realize how insulting that is?"

With a slow, burning thoroughness that scorched through to her bones, his eyes surveyed her from the tip of her head to her moccasin-clad feet. "I suppose it could be an insult at that—if you looked like you did when I met you nine months ago. Right now, you look like a pile of bones with some skin stretched over them—not much for a man to get hold of, honey. And I could wring your neck for cutting off your beautiful hair. What possessed you to to such an inane thing, Sheila?"

"Would you please not lecture me?" she requested stiffly. "It's about as offensive as the rest of your remarks."

He shrugged, then moved with animal grace to the chintz-covered early American sofa and sat down, putting his hands behind his head. "Yes, ma'am," he drawled, and laughed. "Come down off your high horse, little Miss Bag-of-Bones, and sit down and tell

47

me about yourself. I promise to behave, and if you satisfy my curiosity, I'll even promise to go away and leave you alone. I came up here for privacy, too, remember?''

''Then why did you come here?'' she blurted out. ''Come to think of it—how did you know this was my cabin?''

''I know the owners of the other three—except for this little number.'' He glanced around. ''It is small, isn't it? Does it come with indoor plumbing?'' His smile widened at the expression on her face. ''I'm just teasing, Big-Eyes . . . .''

''It's not my place you're making fun of, actually.'' She regarded him with a solemnity that he sensed was too deep to be contrived. ''It belongs to the parents of a friend of mine, and they're letting me use it for the week.''

''Then I take it I'll be rid of you shortly.''

There was a little pause. ''Yes.'' She turned her face aside.

''Hey.'' He rose and came over to the overstuffed recliner where she had sat down. Hunkering down in front of her, he put a hand to her cheek, stroking the delicate cheekbone with his thumb. ''I'm sorry. I hurt your feelings, didn't I?'' His voice was soft, caressing, but when she didn't respond, a frown creased his forehead. ''Sheila? Don't look like that, please. If I'd had any idea you were so sensitive, I would have pulled my punches a little.'' He stood up, staring down at her thoughtfully. ''You know, my memory of you is different from the woman I see before me now. What *did* happen, honey? Tell me about it—then I'll go. Okay?''

His thoughts were blistering, full of self-directed irony. He had never cared before whether or not he hurt somebody's feelings. He had never been deliberately cruel, but other people's feelings were their own problem and, if they didn't like what he had to say, they could stuff it. Now he felt this insane urge to comfort, to wipe away the hurt in her eyes, to hold her in his arms. He wanted to know what had happened, and the need was an irritating spur that goaded him beyond social convention. With a half-audible oath he suddenly reached and hauled her to her feet, tightening the grip when she started to struggle.

"Let me go!" Her voice was a shade away from panic, but it was as much a fear of her body's reaction to his proximity as it was to his aggressiveness. She was aware of him with every nerve, every drop of blood, and her bones seemed to be melting where his hands touched. He released her so suddenly that she stumbled, and glared up at him like a spitting cat.

"Okay—okay." He withdrew a step holding his hands aloft in a mock gesture of surrender. "I get the message . . . I think." He regarded her with sardonic amusement. "No touching on so short an acquaintance, is that it?"

"Not like that, anyway," she fumbled with the arm covers of the chair, keeping her gaze averted. "I'm not used to being mauled."

Cole gave a harsh bark of laughter. "Honey, if I'd intended to maul you, do you think I would have let you go so easily?" His eyes bored into hers as her head flew up to stare at him. "Don't be so blasted gun-shy, woman—I was just trying to get you to snap out of your kicked dog act and talk to me. You're a very irritating female, did you know?"

She was beginning to adjust to his almost brutal frankness, but she still felt the impact of his words, and they stung. "No more than the irritating man you are," she shot back defiantly, but her shoulders were still too set, her lips firmly pressed together.

Cole sighed, muttering an expletive beneath his breath. "Look—I'm sorry. You're right and I promise to try and behave in a more congenial manner in the future." He raked restless fingers through his hair, then turned abruptly and strode over to the door. "I can see that this is definitely not the time, though, so I'll show myself out. Next time, my wary little doe, you can put on a kettle and we'll sip tea and conduct ourselves in a suitably civilized fashion. Will that satisfy you?"

"I didn't mean to over-react." She kept her voice very level, though tell-tale color flayed her cheeks. "And there doesn't even have to be a next time."

"Oh, yes there does," he stated ominously. Then he let himself quietly out the door and was gone.

Sheila spent the rest of the day trying to concentrate on her work and forget about Cole Hampton. By suppertime she had to admit that it was impossible, because she had thrown in the trash every poem she had come up with since he left. She hadn't even been able to compose six lines for a child's birthday card. Finally, she gave up and went to the kitchen to make herself a sandwich. The sun was just setting, and the sky was washed in running shades of pink, lavender and vermilion. It was so breathtaking from the window that Sheila forgot about her sandwich and hurried outside to see it better.

As she made her way down the narrow path that led to the edge of the lake, she kept her eyes glued to the heavenly panorama. Oh, how glorious was the hand of God in nature! There was not a breeze, not any stirring of life, as if all of creation had paused to enjoy the splendor. Like a winking diamond the lake lay in shimmering repose, its surface mirroring the technicolor sky. All around the edges the trees seemed to compete with each other to see which could sprout a different shade of green, with dollops of dogwood intermingled like sprinkles of powdered sugar. Sheila stood very still at the edge of the lake, and for the first time in many months, she was able to thank God for her limited gift of sight. She stayed there, allowing herself to merge with the surroundings as the sun sank slowly behind the trees. Dusky shadows smudged the sky as twilight descended, and, with a contented little murmur, Sheila turned to retrace her steps.

Out of the corner of her eye she noticed some cat-o-nine-tails growing near the water's edge a few yards off the path, and she thought how pretty they would look in a huge blown glass vase she had noticed in the cabin. Busy with thoughts of harvesting her booty and planning how and where to arrange them, she was completely unprepared for the darkness that slammed down. She froze, half-stooped where she had been trying to break off a stem. It was not yet night to the world around her—but it was night to Sheila now and she felt the kick of the shock.

For the first time in eight months she had forgotten about her condition—had forgotten to memorize her surroundings—and now she was as hopelessly disoriented as if she were lost in the middle of the woods. Terror—a snapping, snarling terror that savaged her insides like a mad dog—boiled over and through her so that she trembled with it. She was afraid to move, she was afraid to stay, she was even too frightened to call out. For frozen minutes she didn't move, her hands clutching the forgotten cat-o-nine-tails and her face lifted in stricken anguish of the sky. When a spring pepper suddenly croaked a bare two feet away, she jumped, and lost the last vestiges of control. Hands played before her helplessly, she tore off into the suffocating shroud of blackness—and fell into the lake.

A scream ripped through her throat as the water closed over her in a single, shockingly cold splash. Water flooded her nose, her mouth so that the scream was choked off and turned to a strangled gasp. Oozing mud sucked at her feet and hands as she struggled in vain to rise, and she screamed again.

It could have been seconds, or many minutes, when

the sound of a man's voice dimly penetrated the stygian depths of her nightmare.

"What the—" It was Cole Hampton's voice, and it sounded angry.

Sheila was beyond caring about anything except that there was someone near, someone who could help her. When her arms were encased in iron bands, she reacted wildly, her own arms flailing about as she scrabbled to find something—anything—to hold on to. Through a roaring mist she vaguely heard a muttered curse, then his voice was speaking almost directly in her ear.

"Sheila! What are you trying to pull, anyway? Calm down, now. I've got you . . . ."

There was the sound of splashing and hard breathing as he lifted her into his arms and hauled her out of the lake.

"Sheila!" he snapped again, and she was dumped onto the ground, with one of his arms holding her still, while the other hand clasped her jaw in a strong, almost painful grip. "If you don't calm down I'm going to smack you," he stated in a deadly calm tone that sent anyone who knew him well scurrying for cover.

"P—pl-please . . . don't." She flinched, and with her entire body trembled uncontrollably.

The hand on her chin slid to cup her cheek as his other one rose to join it so that his large hands completely enfolded her face. "Take it easy, honey," he said, and this time his voice was calm, soothing. "It's okay . . . just relax . . . it's okay."

Then his hands were comforting her, wiping the wet hair from her face, her eyes, moving down to her shoulders and stroking with firm, unhurried motions. "Easy, easy, love. You're okay now. Tell me what happened, Sheila. Did something frighten you? How did you fall into the lake?"

She looked blindly up in the direction of his voice,

but her teeth were chattering so convulsively that she couldn't formulate a coherent reply. She heard Cole mutter another curse and then suddenly the world tilted and she was swept into his arms.

"We'll both freeze if we don't get out of these wet clothes," he rasped, and began walking with swift sure strides. "My place is closer. We'll go there."

His steps jarred at first as he seemed to be stepping through weeds and undergrowth. Sheila buried her face in his neck and clung to him with every last scrap of strength. The coolness of the early evening was more like an arctic freeze to her sodden body, except where it made contact with Cole's warmth. He, too, was wet but vitality radiated from him, and his heart beat a strong, steady rhythm next to her. With a shuddering sigh she gave herself over completely to his care, oblivious to circumstances, proprieties or consequences. All she knew was that for the first time since the blindness began, she felt safe.

In a few minutes she felt Cole climbing some steps, then fumbling to open a door. Smells assailed her . . . leather and woodsy smoke . . . some kind of spicy food . . . the merest hint of lemon oil . . . . All of a sudden she was set none too gently on her feet, and the comforting arms were removed.

"The bathroom is down that hall," she heard Cole snap. "There's a robe hanging on the door. Put it on until I find something else you can borrow, and I'll get us something to drink." His voice faded as if he had started to walk away, and Sheila felt more humiliated than she had ever felt in her entire life.

"Cole . . . " she tried to speak, but the word came out as sort of a whispery croak. Her legs were like cold strands of cooked spaghetti, and after taking one fearful step, she had to stop. Tears were very near the surface when his voice exploded from somewhere across the room.

"Get the lead out and move, you little idiot! Or are

you waiting for me to do it for you?'' He was beside her now, his breath warm against her cheek. "Is that what you're angling for, Sheila? Because if it is, you ought to look in a mirror—you look about as seductive as a drowned rat.''

Her eyes, so large and dark and full of anguish, searched the darkness, straining to locate his face through the unrelenting veil.

"Cole,'' she whispered again, and this time she knew he had heard. "I'm sorry, but—but I'm afraid it wouldn't make any difference if I looked in a mirror or not.'' She swallowed the lump of tears. "I can't see anything right now. I'm blind.''

She heard the wind whistle from his lungs in an explosive breath, and then his hand was back on her chin, jerking her face up. "No,'' he breathed, his voice gratingly harsh. "That's impossible! You could see this morning.'' There was a terrible silence, and then the sound of his footsteps walking away. "Oh dear God,'' she heard him groan, and even though Cole Hampton did not have any other marks of a true believer, at this moment his near prayer was convincing. "Sheila . . . . What happened to you?'' With a touch as light as baby's breath, his fingers traced the now sightless eyes, now closed. She could feel her eyelids trembling, and something inside her twisted painfully.

"It happened when I was in that accident last year. There's a small piece of metal . . . floating around in my head. Sometimes it pinches the optic nerve and makes me . . . temporarily blind,'' she faltered, and then her hands were gripped between Cole's so tightly she almost winced. "I never know when it will happen, or how long it will last . . . or whether it might be permanent someday.'' A convulsive shudder jerked through her, and the cold combined with the emotional reaction caused her to sway dizzily. Hard, sinewy arms wrapped about her, held her close, and above her head, Cole muttered agonized curses and self-condemnation. Then he picked her up again and strode down a short hall, stopping a few seconds later.

"This is the bathroom." He placed her down— gently this time—and kept his hands on her shoulder. "If I start the shower and show you where everything is, can you manage?"

"Yes." Her voice was small. His voice sounded brusque, clipped now, as if she were an encumbrance and a nuisance to be rid of as quickly as possible. But then . . . she was blind. What man in his right mind, especially one as active as Cole Hampton, would want anything to do with a blind woman?

"When you're through, call me. I'll guide you back to the den and fix you a drink." There was another terrible pause and she waited, wondering why he didn't leave.

"Sheila . . . ." He started to say more, then with another muffled curse moved past her to start the shower. He showed her how to work the controls, where the towels and his robe were, and then left. The door slammed behind him, and the footsteps that faded rapidly down the hall punctuated his anger.

The hot shower helped. She stood under the pulsing needles of spray for long minutes, just letting the warmth soak into her chilled body, thaw the numbness of her brain. Some of the extremity of her fear gradually faded. A shower was a shower, and she had taken many of them when she had been enduring the attacks of blindness.

Wrapping herself in Cole's soft velour robe was another matter. His scent clung to it, and she felt suddenly overwhelmed by the implied intimacy. She had to put something on, she knew, but the dangers inherent in this kind of situation were just now asserting themselves in all sorts of graphic detail. But she was blind . . . . Propinquity aside, Cole would never dream of forcing himself on a blind woman.

Besides, he had communicated his feelings all too clearly, so without further flutterings, she felt for the doorknob and started moving slowly down the hall, her right hand "seeing" the way before her.

"I thought I told you to call me." Hard hands gripped her shoulders without warning and a shocked gasp whistled past her lips. She flattened herself against the wall she had been using to guide her, totally unaware of the wrenching picture she made. Even when he let her go, she didn't move. "Sheila." His voice drifted over her, as gentle now as a caress. "I'm sorry if I startled you. Hold out your hand, honey."

After a moment she obeyed, and his own hand closed over it, pulling it through his arm as he tugged her with calm strength by his side. "I've started a fire to knock off the chill. Come over here . . . that's it, there's a chair at four o'clock . . . here we go." He eased her down into soft leather cushions, and she felt the heat from the fire on her face and her bare feet, smelled the rich aroma of burning oak, heard the roar and crackle of the flames. A cup was thrust into her hands and then Cole was helping guide it to her lips.

"I can manage," she told him with a slight smile. "I've had quite a bit of practice—oh!" Whatever he had given her was alcoholic and very strong. Sheila wrinkled her nose and held the glass away. "What is this?"

"Brandy. You need something to warm up your insides." He hesitated, and then spoke roughly, "I'm sorry, Sheila. If I'd had any idea . . . you'll never know just how sorry I am . . . . What's the matter?"

"Could—could I please have something else. Some coffee, or tea? I'm not much of a drinker . . . " her voice faded away and then he was lifting the glass from her cold fingers.

"Sure," he said easily, quietly. "I should have known you were a teetotaler, especially since you're a friend of the Allendre's.'' There was a fleeting pat to her shoulder. "Hang loose, little bit of nothing. I'll be back in a few minutes."

Sheila sat back, wondering at his understanding, his gentleness. It was so contradictory to her knowledge of him that she felt oddly lost, as unnerved as she had been that long ago night when they had first been introduced. Over the last several years she had heard snippets now and again of the owner and controlling force behind Hampton Electronics, and none of those snippets had even hinted at any tenderness in his make-up. Even Doris, who never criticized people, had commented on infrequent occasions about Cole's unrelenting drive and insistence on that same unswerving dedication on the part of his employees.

"He's searching for something, I know," she had told Sheila. "Joe says he stays out there in his office sometimes until midnight, working. And he's never idle, never really sits back and kicks off his shoes, so to speak." Her voice had trailed off and she had smiled wistfully at Sheila. "Joe says he can blister a sailor's ears with his language, and the one time Joe said anything about it, he thought Cole would peel a strip off his hide. But you know . . . after that Joe said he was a lot better, especially around Joe . . . . He's a complicated man, Sheila my girl."

If he never took time to relax, then what was he doing up here, Sheila pondered, her hands restlessly stroking the smoothness of the chair arms. What did his house look like? Was he really all alone or did someone come in to help him cook? Had he ever invited a woman here before? The questions darted in and out, as annoying as mosquitoes, but it kept her mind off her own predicament—at least, until Cole came back into the room, the rich aroma of coffee preceding him. He placed a hot mug in her hands and then she heard him sit down somewhere close. Gratefully she raised the hot drink to her lips and took

57

a sip. Her face lifted, staring in his general direction with a wry grimace distorting her features. "All right. What did you put in it?"

"A *touch* of brandy. Don't be difficult—it's purely medicinal and I'm sure your soul won't be in mortal jeopardy."

"I know it won't. And it's not that, anyway—it's the taste."

Cole laughed. "Well, I want every drop inside your stomach, which I'm sure is probably shriveling from starvation anyway. Why aren't you eating properly? It wouldn't take more than a puff of wind to blow you away."

Sheila took a careful sip of the bitter coffee. "I haven't had much appetite lately," she admitted.

"Tell me about the blindness. When did it start— has an operation been suggested?"

"What is this, an inquisition?" She took another swallow, then felt around until she found the table beside the chair. Setting the mug down, she lifted her hands to her eyes, pressing them against her lids in one of the gestures Hannah nagged at her about. The last thing she felt like doing was discussing her personal problems with Cole Hampton, especially right now when she was so defenseless.

She just KNEW he already considered her a baby, an irrational, babbling idiot for behaving as she had. Screaming, falling in the lake . . . and now he wanted to dig in the knife a little deeper by demanding to know all the painful details of the past. Never in all these last endless months had Sheila felt quite so low. She was sitting in a house she had never seen, wearing nothing but a man's robe, and the man was not exactly known for his Christian values . . . and she was blind.

"Sheila, I really would like to know." His voice was quiet, the tone so sincere and devoid of any of the normal mockery that she found herself responding with surprising naturalness.

"I had the first—episode—the day after the crash. They ran all sorts of tests, called in specialists from all over—(even under rocks, it seemed like at the time). Everyone but one doctor from Duke, I think, agreed that an operation was too risky. I just had to learn to live with it and make the best of things."

"You don't look like you've been doing that," he commented with cool precision.

Her chin lifted. "No," she agreed, and her sightless eyes didn't even flicker, "I guess I haven't exactly come off too well in this particular trial, but I will eventually." A will-o-the-wisp grin flitted across the soft contours of her mouth. "I may be down, but I'm not quite out—even if I *do* look like a drowned rat and a bag of bones."

Cole chuckled softly, the sound teasing her senses pleasantly. "I've never been known for my tact, but beautiful women usually don't have any complaints about my descriptions of them." He paused, then added musingly, "Last August you were the most intriguing woman I'd ever seen, and I was determined to initiate a relationship—a very *close* relationship. I used to dream about your hair, all long and soft and flowing . . . and your eyes. I could lose myself in the laughter I saw in your eyes, Sheila Jamison. What happened to that woman—is it the accident, the blindness that killed her?"

There was something in his voice—some undercurrent she couldn't fathom—and it caused her to stir restlessly in her chair. Her fingers groped for the mug and she took a couple of sips to steel herself against a nebulous uneasiness. "That woman had never had anything happen to—to kill the laughter before. I could even accept the death of both my parents several years ago because I knew that they would be together and happy for always." She sighed. "I suppose I was riding for a fall." The threat of tears was back, and she fought to swallow them down. "I

59

guess I'm not exactly the best example of a trusting Christian right now, and that hurts more than anything else." Her head turned toward Cole bravely, and the eyes were haunted, dark with shadows. "Did you even know that I'm a Christian, Cole?" She could almost hear the shrug as he answered.

"So? I never really thought about it one way or the other. When I met you last year, your brand of religion was not exactly the thing uppermost in my mind."

Sheila very carefully set the mug down. "Well, whatever you might have been thinking can just be forgotten." she replied very quietly. "Regardless of what today's society condones, I won't be following the crowd. I *am* still a Christian, however weak I feel right now, and I won't be going to bed with any man unless and until he's my husband."

"You tempt me to make you eat those words . . . ."

She stood, fumbling for the chair and clutching the robe, suddenly aware of her vulnerability. He was too blunt, too sophisticated for her and far too dangerous. What was he thinking right now? If she could only see, she would be able to read his eyes, guage his expression. Was he teasing—or, heaven help her—was he serious?.

When he took her by the shoulders she erupted, twisting, kicking out with her leg as her hands beat at his chest and shoulders. "No! Don't touch me!" Any other words were crowded down her throat as his mouth covered hers. He wasn't brutal, or even particularly passionate, but with his kiss stemming her cries and his arms pinning her helplessly, she was unable to do anything. With a yielding sob she relaxed, and he lifted his head immediately.

"That's the best way I know to shut up a hysterical woman," he growled softly into her ear. "Hush now, Sheila. I'm not going to hurt you. Just . . . be still." He was still holding her, but loosely now, and his hands were rubbing up and down her arms, quieting her like a skittish mare.

Her mouth was tingling from the touch. She felt as if someone had set off sizzling sparklers and they were zinging from her toes to her nose. She had never, ever felt this way about a man before and she didn't know how to deal with it. Deeply ingrained into her very being was the desire to remain pure and chaste, keeping for her husband the most precious gift God gave a woman to symbolize the dimensions of earthly love. She had no intention of giving into the current attitude that said if it felt good, do it . . . but why was her body clammoring for his touch? What would she do if he kissed her like he meant it, with passion and tenderness and desire? Would all her lifelong values, her Christian faith, be strong enough to combat the tidal wave of feeling that Cole Hampton was able to create?

"Sheila . . . ." His fingers touched her mouth gently, and his voice was soft with warning. "I realize you feel helpless right now, but blind or not, you need to control the expression in these big brown eyes and this soft little mouth. I've never had to practice restraint with women before, honey, so I'll need some help."

"But how am I looking at you?" She couldn't help it—she had to ask, even when she instinctively knew she wouldn't like the answer.

"Like you want to be kissed—-thoroughly. Like you'll melt into me if I hold you close." With a suddenness that left her gaping, he thrust her back into the chair, smothering a curse as he roughly drew the lapels of the robe closer together. "You also look like a motherless fawn staring down the barrel of a gun, so what's a guy supposed to do?" Sheila heard him pacing, then take a hard swallow of whatever he was drinking. "Stay here by the fire and try to relax. I'll go check on supper and see if your clothes are dry. Maybe then the world won't look so black."

He was gone before Sheila could point out the irony of those words, so she lay back in the chair, closing her eyes with a long sigh. Right now she was just too exhausted, physically and emotionally, to fight with Cole Hampton. She would just have to trust him to be a—a gentleman. It was with a queer wrench of her heart that she suddenly realized she *did* trust him somehow; that in spite of his abrasive words and sometimes aggressive actions toward her, she instinctively knew he was not going to hurt or shame her.

A tiny little imp of the old Sheila reared its head briefly as she thought about some of the less than flattering appellations he had applied to her—*rat, bag of bones*. What exactly *would* it take to hurt and shame her if that didn't do the trick? There was a wistful little smile on her face as she slid into a sound sleep, lulled by the fire, the hot coffee, and an aura of peace and safety she was too bemused to grasp at the moment.

Cole stared down at her for a long time, his eyes caressing the shadows and hollows of her face created by the fire. The dark halo of hair had dried into fuzzy ringlets that fell in soft disarray all over her head. His hand lifted instinctively to touch it, then dropped, and a bleakness came into his eyes along with a sort of pain. Guilt twisted his mouth into a grimace as it twisted his insides in knots.

Blind. Blind. The word had been pinging around his head ever since she told him, and it had taken all his considerable self-control to keep from slamming his fist through the wall. Why couldn't it have been some other poor slob he had to hit that night instead of her? Why hadn't her God been watching out for her?

He thought of the Allendres, how supportive they had been after the crash even though it was his fault. They had never condemned him, never acted like he had done anything wrong—even after they obviously must have known about the blindness. Joe had always been unflappable, competent, even reassuring Cole that everything would work out okay and that he needn't worry about Sheila. She was being well cared for . . . .

At the time, it had just been so many words, but now he stared down at the fragile shell of a girl and wanted to curse the God she and the Allendres seemed to trust so much. Then, like a meteor arching across the sky, came a memory that was going on fifteen years old. He was in Viet Nam, and one of his closest friends had caught a head full of shrapnel. Although his buddy would survive, he would be permanently blind. Cole, his guts twisting in agony, had gone to visit him at the base hospital in Bien Hoa. Danny had been sitting up in the bed, his head swathed in white bandages, but a serene smile on his face.

"Don't you worry about me, buddy," he had said to Cole, his voice strong and cheerful. "I've got my life, and the good Lord will see me through. He'll be right by my side, Cole, just like He's always been. Sight doesn't make or break a guy, you know. There are a lot of people walking around with two good eyes who are more blind than I am . . . ."

Cole hadn't seen Danny after that; his unit was shipped to Da Nang, and Danny had been transferred to a hospital in Okinawa, and even though he hadn't consciously thought of his friend in years, he realized he was comparing him to Sheila now. If Danny could react with a serenity that went beyond the rational, claiming it was God, then why couldn't Sheila?

She had said she was a Christian, and there was certainly an air about her—something that registered almost subconsciously—that made her radically different from all the other women he had desired. But he had seen her fear, heard her somehow poignant confession, been shocked by the changes in her. What

63

was it she had said—that she had never had anything happen to her to kill the laughter?

Well, she obviously hadn't been down the road he had, and it was just as obvious she was suffering for it now. He was curious, and stubbornly refused to examine why, to pursue the matter, to probe her mind and see just exactly what she meant when she said she was a Christian. He had heard the term applied to all sorts of people in all walks of life, in a vast array of situations, over his admittedly non-Christian life. As far as he could tell, the vast majority of them didn't seem to be any different from him, and a lot were worse. But then there was Danny . . . Joe and Doris Allendre . . . and now Sheila herself. What did it all mean?

She woke slowly, her nose telling her that somewhere there was some food that smelled delicious But the world was still a dark void, and her hands reached in the automatic gesture to rub her eyes.

"It's about time," Cole's voice came out of the darkness, deep and faintly teasing. "You'll probably have a tough time getting to sleep tonight after a nap like that."

"How long did I sleep?" Her voice was still drowsy, and she was so deliciously warm she didn't want to move. Everything was unreal, surrealistic, like there was a fuzzy film over all her other senses.

"A little over an hour. Long enough for your clothes to dry and for me to whip up a supper to whet even your scrawny appetite."

"You—you cooked a meal?" She felt the heat in her cheeks at that gauche and incredulous question, and it burned hotter when he laughed.

"Did you think I had to have someone do it for me if it was more elaborate than opening a can or sticking a TV dinner in the oven?" His hands lifted her gently to her feet with nothing but courteous solicitude.

"Believe it or not, in my long and somewhat question-able life, I've done a few things besides keep a multi-million dollar firm solvent. Being a short order cook at a twenty-four hour restaurant was one of them. Careful—there's the doorway. That's it. Here's the bathroom."

After she had changed back into her own clothes, she felt a lot better, although she was still nervous and uneasy around Cole. She soon realized there was no need to be. With the lightest of touches, he guided her back to a room where supper was waiting, and throughout the meal he treated her with a matter-of-factness that gradually lulled her into almost complete relaxation. He had steered her hands over the table to identify all the utensils, then described the food on her plate, using the hands on the clock to position the items. It was as if he had dealt with blind people every day.

"How do you do it?" she had asked at one point, and she heard the answering grin in his voice. "Do what?"

"Act like you don't really notice that I'm blind. And when you do, you don't treat me like a freak or an imbecile. Have you known someone who was blind?"

"Only one," he replied, thinking of Danny, "and I only saw him once after he was blinded." He took a bite of the stuffed flounder and then remarked, "I'm not an imbecile, either, you know, and it only takes a little bit of common sense to figure out that you need to be treated as naturally as possible, especially under your somewhat stressful circumstances. How long are you usually blind before your sight returns?"

Sheila lifted her shoulders, carefully setting her fork down on her plate. "A couple of hours to a couple of days. Right after I got here, I had one spell that lasted only twenty minutes, but I never know."

His voice came at her like a battering ram. "Who

let you come up here by yourself? You're crazy, you know! What would have happened if I hadn't been outside and heard you scream? You must be out of your mind!"

"I will be—if I don't learn how to cope on my own." She kept her hands clenched tightly in her lap so he couldn't see their trembling. "Can you possibly imagine what it's like? It's like living on a tightrope that's fraying, and I never know when the last strand will go. I can't drive a car. I can't even go to the store with the confidence that I'll be able to buy everything I need before the next one hits. And, on top of that, I have a whole army of friends who won't even let me *try* to learn a little independence. The lady who lives with me now doesn't even want me to walk across the street if she's not watching. I was suffocating, Cole. I've lost my freedom, my confidence, even my ability to write." She took a shuddering breath. "And I seem to have lost my trust in God. I know you don't understand that, but one of the reasons I came here was to try and find that part of me you met back in August. And I can't do it with someone hovering over me twenty-four hours a day like I was a fledgling chick. I call Hannah every night to check in—but, I've been here almost a week now, and I'm still alive."

"Barely," he shot a rejoinder.

"Yes, well, I do have you to thank for that." Her voice was a little sheepish, but still determined. "It won't happen again, though. I've learned my lesson and won't be traipsing around unless I've memorized the way back to my cabin. Which reminds me—could you take me home now? The supper was delicious but . . . ."

"Then why didn't you finish it?"

" —but I've taken up too much of your time as it is. I promise not to take any more impromptu dips in the lake, and if you'll tell me when you jog and take your

66

walks, I'll time mine different. You won't have to bother with me anymore.''

"Are you quite finished?'' he inquired very gently. Her skin prickling, Sheila nodded bravely.

"You've made a token protest and the grand gesture—okay. Consider your conscience clear. But it will be a cold day in July before I allow you to go back to your cabin in this condition. You'll be staying here with me until your sight comes back. And then either you call your friend to come and get you, or I'll take you home myself.'' His voice was so calm, so even, that it took a minute for the import of the words to register.

"You have no right,'' she began, her voice shaking.

"Who's going to stop me?'' he cut off the protest pleasantly, then rose and advanced toward her. "Sheila, use your head. You can't stay in that cabin by yourself when you can't see, and you can't expect me to just dump you there and forget about you.''

"Why not? You came up here to be alone, you said. And I don't want to stay here—it's not right.'' She had to clear her throat, and even then the words sounded alarmingly feeble. "Please, Cole. Take me back. I'll be all right.''

With infinitely gentle hands, he lifted her from the chair, held her close. "No,'' he murmured next to her ear, and his breath stirred the silky wisps of hair, sending shivers cascading down her spine. "No, baby. You might as well resign yourself—you're staying here.''

CHAPTER 4

SHE THOUGHT ABOUT STRUGGLING, but she knew with bitter resignation that she would only end up being humiliated. She thought about letting loose the storm of tears that were welling up behind her eyes and crowding her throat, but she had always felt that using tears as emotional blackmail was contemptible. And then she thought—really thought—about sharing this house with Cole, and she felt stark terror.

"I can't stay here," she repeated, her voice muffled against the soft fabric of his shirt. Her arms had come up, her hands clutching his shoulders and feeling the tensile strength of the powerful muscles. If he wanted to he could crush her, but he was being so very gentle .... "Cole, if I stay here I would have the same problem I had back home. How can I learn to cope on my own if you're dogging my every step to catch me if I stumble?"

"What would you have done if I hadn't been there to catch your 'stumble' into the lake?"

She lifted her head, and her wide unblinking eyes were poignantly beseeching. "All right—I told you I know I panicked. But I would have been able to get myself out in a minute, and it really wasn't deep enough there to drown. I've already made a fool of myself. Please understand that I *need* to learn how to be independent. I won't always have you . . . or anyone else . . . ." Her voice trailed away in confusion as she realized how pathetic she must sound.

He loosened his grip, allowing her a measure of space, but his hands kept a comforting grip on her shoulders.

Sheila, listen to me now. I do understand what you're saying, and I think I can even understand a little of how you feel." He paused, and she could hear the smile in his next words. "But I also know how *I* feel, and if I let you go, I won't sleep, and *that*, my little fledgling chick, is not an advisable state of affairs."

"Well, I won't sleep if I have to stay here, either," she flashed, and then a sheepish grin lifted the corners of her mouth. "I do hope you aren't planning to offer any remedies that would offend my tender sensibilities . . . ."

Cole laughed outright at that, and his fingers brushed ever so lightly against her cheek. "I don't think I'd touch that one with a ten-foot pole." There was the sound of dishes being stacked and silverware clattering. "Help me clean the kitchen. That will give you time to come to terms with the way it's going to be—my way—and it will also give you a chance to prove how proficient you are when you're blind."

With a lift of her chin she accepted his challenge, her hands reaching down to the table to feel gingerly around. "First you'll have to show me the phone so I can check in with Hannah. If I don't call every evening she'd be up in an hour, and I won't be demonstrating any proficiency except how fast I pack clothes."

Cole obeyed, and she heard him chuckling softly as

she gritted her teeth and assured Hannah she was quite all right. It was the truth, after all, even if it wasn't quite *all* the truth. "Now you'll have to show me where the sink is," she stated calmly, after hanging up, and felt his hands come round her waist to guide her back across the floor.

She surprised both of them with her adeptness, and Sheila couldn't help but toss a self-satisfied grin in Cole's direction as she finished drying the last plate. "Now, if you'll just point me to the door," she tried, keeping her voice light and oh-so-careless.

"Certainly," Cole answered immediately, much too genially for Sheila's peace of mind. "This way." He drew her arm through his and led her out of the kitchen.

Sheila stopped abruptly. "This is the hall to the bathroom," she stated flatly a minute later.

"Also the rest of the house," was the cheerful rejoinder. "I'm showing you to the door, Sheila—but it's the door to your bedroom."

"If I took a swing at you, would you duck before it connected?"

"Don't be cute."

"How about two out of three?" She couldn't help it, her voice was rising and she knew she was trembling as well. He must think her the silliest female alive. Then his voice spoke from right above her ear, and the tones were deep as chocolate, soothing as a balm.

"Honey, take it easy. You're acting like an hysterical little prude. I confess my experience is limited with ladies of your persuasion, but that doesn't mean I'm going to sweep you into my arms and toss you on the nearest bed for the sole purpose of depriving you of that rarefied status."

The tone might have been soothing, but the words were more of a liniment. "I wish you wouldn't be so sarcastic," she said, swallowing hard. "It isn't kind."

"I'm not particularly known for my kindness," Cole returned evenly, "and I think any other attitude at this point is going to provoke the tears you're trying so hard to keep from shedding in my presence." He tugged her almost roughly into a room, then pushed her onto a firm bed. "I'll let you explore your prison by yourself to keep you from getting the wrong idea about my motives. I'll be right across the hall if you need anything."

Biting on her bottom lip, hands burrowing into the heavy-textured bedspread, Sheila spent the next minutes trying to keep from drowning in self-pity and confusion. She felt trapped, helpless, and floundering in the wake of Cole Hampton's abrupt moods. It was almost as if he had been softening her up for the killing blow, which she felt he had just administered with a bludgeon. What was worse, she knew that she had no choice but to stay here, because there was no way she could possibly find her way back to her cabin, and the thought of being lost outside in the darkness was even more terrifying than losing herself in the darkness of Cole's personality.

After awhile, with slow and faltering steps she rose to explore the confines of the room. The furniture felt heavy and expensive, with a silky-smooth finish that was somehow strangely pleasant to her fingertips. It wasn't a large room, and besides the bed, contained only the standard nightstand, bureau, and dresser, along with what seemed to be a contemporary styled chair beneath a window. She wondered what the colors were, what patterns he had used. Was it a masculine, or feminine room? Dark or light?

"Sheila?"

His voice sounded muffled, so he must have shut the door on his way out. Sheila was standing on the other side of the room, and she stayed there, her breathing light and fast. "What do you want?"

"Are you okay?" There was a reluctant concern in

the words that almost made her smile. He obviously didn't like having her as a responsibility any more than she liked being one.

"I'm fine."

There was a short pause. "Do you want to borrow one of my T-shirts to sleep in?" Now she could hear the laughter back in his voice. Sheila was profoundly glad that he wasn't attempting to open the door, because she knew her face was probably the color of an overripe tomato.

"No. Go away." Her voice betrayed her discomfort, and she heard him chuckle, a very amused masculine chuckle that made her want to hit him again.

"Come on, Sheila, don't be silly. If it would make you feel better, I'll just throw it through the door with my eyes *closed.*"

"Very well," she replied at last, her voice hesitant. "And you don't have to throw it through the door."

She waited, listening to the sound of the door opening and his footsteps strolling with casual purpose into the room. Her back was to him, she knew, and she prayed that he would just toss the garment on the bed and walk out. She should have known better.

"You're crying." His thumb brushed the drops that had slipped in mute disobedience down her cheeks, and she felt his breath inhale sharply, heard him mutter something beneath his breath.

"I'm sorry." She kept her chin high, eyes open.

"No—*I'm* sorry," he apologized roughly. "I shouldn't have teased you like that." He placed the shirt in her hands, holding onto hers a minute before releasing them. "It's a h—, it's a bad situation all around, honey, but that was no excuse for taking it out on you. If I promise to watch what I say in the future, will you give me one of your beautiful smiles to sleep on?"

Now it was Sheila who inhaled sharply, and there

72

was a moment of crystalline silence where she felt poised on the brink of an abyss. Then, her mouth curving upwards in a tremulous smile, she whispered, "Thank you for the shirt. You're really a very kind man."

"Sheila," he groaned, and his hands descended heavily on her shoulders. He pulled her to him and hugged her briefly before thrusting her away with an abruptness that she knew was not intentional. "Call me if you need me. Promise me, Sheila."

"I promise." She was twisting the T-shirt in her hands, and those sparklers were sizzling again.

"Goodnight," he bit out, and then she heard him stalk away. This time the door was shut very definitely.

She woke up quite suddenly. Moonlight was spilling onto the bed through the floor-to-ceiling windows. *I guess I forgot to draw the drapes*, Sheila thought in dismay.

It took a moment for the reality to register, but when it did, she gave an incoherent muffled cry of utter relief. She could see! She gazed around the room in almost tearful wonder, her heart beating in heavy thuds. Joy and gratitude filled her, and she jumped hastily from the bed to stand at the window, gazing out into the night with rapt intensity. She had learned very painfully not to take her sight for granted, and each time she plowed her way through a period of total darkness, she found herself growing more appreciative of the gift of sight. If only she didn't have to live with the constant fear of losing it again.

With curious eyes, she wandered around the room, turning on the lamp by the bed so that she could see better. It was an impersonal room, without any real clues as to Cole's personality. The furniture, as she suspected, was of top quality, but the contemporary style and the neutral colors were disappointing. She would have thought he had, well, a bolder and more adventurous taste.

Something like pain twisted her insides as she imagined in vivid detail how he would look, what he would say in the morning when he rose to find that Sheila could see again. With his scathing brand of humor, he might even accuse her of staying, with the hope of playing on his sympathies.

She realized suddenly that there would be no reason for her to stay here now, and how relieved that would undoubtedly make Cole. With an abruptness totally out of character, Sheila decided not to wait until morning to leave. She would find her way back to her cabin right now, tonight, and maybe she could avoid any further awkwardness with Cole.

Whipping off the T-shirt that was so large it fell halfway down her legs, she found herself staring at it for an agonized moment before tossing it on the bed. She dressed hurriedly, turned out the light and opened the door, her heart beating somewhere in her throat as she tiptoed past Cole's room and down the hall. It was too dark to see the details of the house, and she had to admit to herself that she preferred leaving as blind as she had come. Any more visual memories would only make the whole experience harder to forget.

Moving as furtively as a wary cat, she edged her way to the front door and drew back the deadbolt, her hands shaking. What if it made a noise? Then she was safely outside in the chill of the spring night, with the moon shining benignly down and bathing the world in silver. For a frantic moment she hesitated, not knowing which way to go, but the image of Cole Hampton's undisguised relief was a spur that goaded her to movement.

She knew the general direction of his house from her cabin, so all she had to do was find the path and follow it home. The moonlight helped, and by the time her eyes adjusted to the darkness—only it wasn't, would never be the total darkness she had known in those terrifying periods of absolute blindness—she could pick out the break in the trees and the path beckoning her decidedly rubbery limbs. Like the heroine in a Victorian melodrama, she fled silently, sadly, with the bitter knowledge of her cowardice snapping at her heels.

He didn't even have the courtesy to wait until after breakfast to hunt her down. Sheila had just risen and put on some water for coffee when the cabin shook with thunderous knocking.

"Open this door, you foolish, aggravating, idiotic woman!" he demanded with such bone-chilling deliberateness that Sheila found herself obeying.

"Why are you here?" she asked inanely when she opened the door, and that was when she noticed the vein beating heavily in his temple and the line of white scoring his face deeply on either side of his nose. Involuntarily she stepped back. "I guess that was a stupid question, wasn't it?"

"Stupid question from a stupid woman," he ground out with deliberate offense. He followed her, stalking her like the panther she had once whimsically compared him to. "Do you have any idea—*any* idea—of my feelings when I woke up and found you gone? No note, no nothing but a T-shirt that was minus a body?" He glared at her, the look flicking at her like steel knives. "I learned a few years ago to keep a lid on my temper, Sheila Jamison, but right now you're doing a fair job of blowing that lid to—" his mouth twisted in a sardonic grin, "—'Hades' and back."

"I thought you'd be glad to get rid of me." She moved again, this time placing a huge rocking chair between herself and the angry man. "You came here to be alone, you said. You didn't want anyone, especially female, invading your privacy and your peace." She gazed back, uncertainty swimming in the big brown eyes as she struggled to comprehend his anger.

"You could have left a note at least," he growled, one corner of his mouth lifting again at Sheila's blush.

"I didn't think of that," she admitted. "I was so relieved to be able to see that all I could think of was getting home and leaving you alone."

"You were in such an all-fired hurry, you couldn't even wait until morning? What time did you make your insane escape, anyway?"

"Uh—about two-thirty. I woke up and I could see and I—I just dressed and left."

"Why didn't you wait until morning, Sheila?" Some of the anger had dissipated, but that question made her even more uneasy.

"I told you—I was trying to get out of your hair and leave you alone. You made it quite plain that I was an unwelcome burden."

He advanced upon her again, a look in the darkening gray eyes that sent her scuttling backward like a skittish crab. He reached out a casual hand and caught her arm. "Is that really your interpretation, my frightened little doe?"

"Y-yes."

"You're a little liar." He pulled her into a loose embrace that was nevertheless unbreakable. "Or you're extremely dense. Which means—since I'm not attracted to women with those characteristics—that, in reality, you're neither a liar nor dense." He smiled with devilish charm down into her eyes. "It means you're attracted to me like I am to you, and you're scared to death." His hands moved lightly down her arms. "Have you ever felt like that about any man before, Sheila?"

"A baker's dozen," she snapped, pushing at his chest. "Has anyone ever told you how arrogant and conceited you are?"

"Frequently. Be still—I'm not quite in control of

76

my baser emotions and when you struggle like that, you're asking for trouble."

"You won't lose control though," Sheila murmured, her face blooming like a summer rose, "*Will* you?"

He stared down at her, stared so long and deeply that it was as if he were climbing into her brain and prying loose all its secrets. Then he swore, releasing her and raking impatient fingers through his uncombed hair. "No . . . . But if you don't stop looking at me with those cow-eyes and your mouth all soft and trembling, I swear I won't be responsible." He speared her with a stabbing glance. "And I don't stop with chaste kisses anymore, honey. Do you understand?"

"I'm not sixteen, *Mr*. Hampton." Her own eyes fell, because although she was not naive, she was also not used to having such a frankly sexual discussion. She was also having a problem with her unruly and rebellious body, which was in fact clamoring for his kisses, chaste or not. Temptation had never presented itself in this particular guise. She had always felt that even when she fell in love, she would want to be virgin on her wedding night. She still planned to be, but she was beginning to understand why she was—as Cole had said—an uncommon species nowadays. It would be perilously easy . . . .

"What are you thinking?"

Scarlet swept up from her throat to her hairline. "Nothing that you need to hear," she choked out. "Would you—would you like a cup of coffee before you go?"

He cocked his head to one side, pondering her a minute before he replied, "Yes, I'll share a cup of coffee with you . . . before I go."

She added more water and another tablespoon of the rich coffee to the filter, unable to suppress the thought that it was almost as dark and rich as Cole's hair. When it had perked, she poured two cups, and they drank in a silence that grew rapidly more strained.

Cole looked infuriatingly relaxed, sitting in the kitchen chair with his long legs lounging casually out into the middle of the floor as he slowly sipped the hot liquid. Sheila was sitting straight and rigid, and the longer Cole went without speaking, the more fidgety she grew. He finished the cup, placed it decisively on the table and rose.

"Thanks. I enjoyed that." Then, without another word he started walking out of the room toward the front door.

Sheila followed him, stopping at the entrance to the kitchen when he turned back after opening the door. "You know, you look a lot more alive than you did a few days ago. I guess that's something, anyway." The words might have been flung carelessly over his back, but they found their target with deadly accuracy.

Sheila spent the rest of the morning in troubled introspection, wandering around the little cabin with aimless movements, unable to sit still. Cole had definitely made a dent in the murky fog of apathy and despair in which she had been existing for the last eight months. But she really didn't need that kind of complication. She wanted, if she were honest with herself, a handwritten message from the angel Gabriel himself, telling her that everything would be all right, that God would be intervening on a particular date, and she would once again be the Sheila Jamison she had been a year ago. What she *didn't* want was to find herself attracted to a man who used words like weapons and his potent masculinity as the *coup de grace*.

"I came up here to find my faith again," she announced aloud just to hear the conviction in her voice. "I didn't come up here to find myself more confused than ever by some wretchedly attractive man—who goes out of his way to be cold and brutal to me one minute, then turns right around and all but cherishes me."

That afternoon she went for a short walk around the perimeter of the cleared land on which the cabin sat. There was a heavy wetness in the air, and the breeze that occasionally teased her short curls smelled of rain. Glancing up into the sky, Sheila could see the clouds building behind the trees, moving even as she strolled to block out the brilliant blue. There would be a spring shower or two by nightfall—maybe even a thunderstorm. Well, that was all right with her. She wasn't frightened by storms and the pitter-patter of the falling raindrops was actually soothing. Remnants of songs about rain floated unbidden into her head, and a wistful smile crossed her face very briefly. It had been a long time since she had yielded to whatever imp it was that provoked her into a burst of off-key singing. Had Cole brought that back to life, too? She shook her head, enjoying the coolness of the riding wind, and almost in spite of herself began humming. She was just starting to climb the steps to the cabin when she glanced up to see Cole, sitting in the rocker on the porch, looking very much as if he belonged there.

"It looks like we'll be having rain tonight," he offered, stretching his legs and propping an arm on the rocker with his hand supporting his chin. "I thought I'd come see if you were afraid of storms."

"No." She climbed the rest of the steps slowly, stood looking down at him with something like resigned despair.

"Okay—I came because *I'm* afraid of storms and wanted your company."

Her face relaxed into a smile at last. "If I believed in tit for tat, I'd be calling you a liar. I don't think you've ever been afraid of anything."

"Only a fool is never afraid." He rose and pondered her somberly. "I've been afraid lots of times in my life. The difference between you and me, Sheila Jamison, is that I've learned how to conquer my fears, while you are letting yours conquer *you*."

She flushed, and didn't reply, because she knew it was the truth.

"Have you eaten supper?" As if he sensed he had hit a raw nerve, Cole shifted to neutral ground, his devastating smile coaxing her to do likewise.

"At five o'clock? What time do you usually eat?"

"Whenever I get hungry," he replied, unabashed. "That's the nice thing about being a bachelor. I do what I want when I want and don't have to worry about anyone trying to run my life."

Sheila was still slightly raw from his stinging observations. "Then, don't let *me* interfere. I'm not hungry, and I'm not afraid of the weather, so feel free to return to your solitary retreat and do as you please."

She started to walk on beyond him, feeling ashamed of her outburst, but finding herself quite unable to apologize. Lately her temper had been as short and frayed as a worn-out rope, and Cole Hampton's irritating presence in her life was only aggravating it further. So she avoided looking at him, and was turning the doorknob when his hand closed over hers.

"I can take a hint," he remarked calmly, his voice wry, "but if your sight goes again, will you promise to call me?"

His last words seemed to punch into her heart and send it slamming against her ribs. She swallowed, realizing at only that very moment that she had subconsciously wanted to do exactly that. So much for independence. "I don't know your phone number," she submitted, keeping her voice very level.

"It's unlisted. I'll write it down for you and then I want you to memorize it. Okay?"

She pushed open the door and walked inside, her feet dragging. "I'll think about it."

He had followed her in and moved with his usual sleek economy and grace to the card table, helping himself to a clean sheet of typing paper. With rapid strokes he wrote out the number, and strode back over to Sheila. "Do it," he commanded with consummate arrogance, stuffing the slip in her shirt pocket.

Sheila flinched at the brief but intimate contact and her eyes flashed daggers. Cole merely laughed and kept walking.

"See you later," he promised softly, just as the first rumble of thunder echoed in the distance.

The storm swept over the lake with the wanton abandon of spring storms, blowing in with reverberating claps of thunder and crackling flashes of lightning. It moved on just as abruptly, leaving behind a steady drizzle that finally succeeded in lulling Sheila to sleep.

Cole spent the next few days dreaming up, in Sheila's exasperated opinion, new and infuriating ways to further aggravate her. If he wasn't just "dropping by" to see how she was doing, he was issuing a constant stream of invitations that ran the gamut from dinner at his place to spending the day in the mountains. He tired to wangle invitations for himself, too, timing his appearances to coincide with her mealtimes. He called on the phone, with his most persuasive arguments as to why jog with him, go canoeing on the lake . . . and made a complete and utter pest of himself.

Sheila found her amusement at his blatant tactics warring with the irritation. Strangely he never forced her acceptance. Every time she refused his offers, he yielded graciously, though occasionally she detected a certain gleam in the back of his eyes that promised retribution. But for some reason she couldn't fathom, he had chosen to sheathe his own formidable temper, using the just as formidable power of his charm. Once Sheila found herself starting to succumb, she called Hannah.

"I'm ready to come home," she announced without preamble, and waited for the reaction.

"Are you having a spell?" Hannah asked. She had never come right out and asked before, and Sheila was deeply appreciative of her forbearance.

"No. I . . . I just want to come home. I've finished all the work I brought with me and need to start on the artwork. Remember, I didn't bring any of my supplies up here." Actually, she was surprised at the ease with which she had been able to compose the last few days, in spite of Cole's interference. "Can you come and get me now? I'll be packed by the time you get here."

"I have a pound cake in the oven that's due to come out in thirty minutes, but I can leave after that. Sheila?"

"Don't question me now, Hannah. I've made it through a week, but I decided not to stay longer." Her fingers worried through the rumpled curls, moved to rub her eyes. "I'll see you in a couple of hours, okay?"

Now if she could just pack, clean the cabin and not have a spell. . . . And if Cole would stay away so she wouldn't have the problem of explaining. Of course, she really didn't intend to leave without any word at all. She had already done that to him once; it wouldn't be fair. Besides, she hadn't cared for his reaction, and if she callously disappeared without so much as a note, he would more than likely mete out the kind of punishment he had only threatened before. Keeping one eye on the clock and the other on the window, she quickly, methodically filled her one suitcase, swept, dusted and straightened, breathing freely only when she had finished her chores and she could still see. There was still no sign of Cole.

The note was difficult to write. She didn't want to sound too impersonal and polite, but neither did she want to sound like she was hinting at a depth of feeling that didn't exist. "And I certainly don't want to make it sound like I'm hoping he'll look me up when he gets back in town," she mumbled as she chewed on the end of her pen. Several sheets of paper were crumpled and tossed in the wastebasket before she felt halfway satisfied. After rummaging in the kitchen drawer for some tape, she carefully fastened the note on the front door where he couldn't possibly miss it. Then she sat down to wait for Hannah.

CHAPTER 5

"WELL, I HATE TO ADMIT IT but you do look better than when I brought you up here." Hannah glanced over at her again as they drove down a winding road that connected to the main highway.

"That's what I'd call a real backhanded compliment," Sheila mused, smiling across at the older woman before turning to gaze out the window.

"Sheila. . . ." Hannah paused, and Sheila felt her muscles knotting at the obvious hesitation. "I want to know if you had any spells," she blurted out quickly at last. "I haven't asked because I quite frankly was afraid to, but now that you're here and all right, I've just got to know."

Sheila sighed, and forced herself to reply calmly. "Two minor ones," she admitted. "One lasted only twenty minutes. The other one—" Her hands clenched into fists, but when she saw Hannah observing this revealing mannerism, she opened them to rest unmoving in her lap. "The other one lasted a couple of hours. I went to bed blind, woke up in the middle of the night, and I could see. No problems, no—catastrophes, and as you can *see* for yourself, I'm just fine." *Only I can't talk about meeting Cole. I can't tell you what happened, or you'll lock me in my room and never let me out by myself again.*

She couldn't help remembering how Cole had—in spite of all his irritating appearances on her doorstep—always left her alone when she insisted. He had allowed her the breathing space she so desperately needed, even though Sheila knew he hadn't liked to. Of course, the reason he hadn't liked it might possibly have been because she hadn't fallen at his feet like all the other women he knew. Maybe it wasn't concern for her attacks of blindness at all. Maybe it was ego and determination to turn her into one more conquest, one more notch for his belt. What *did* Cole Hampton want from her?

"What are you thinking about, with such a frown on your face?" Hannah's curious voice intruded into her painful introspective musings, and Sheila came back to reality with a jolt. "Are you being entirely honest with me, Sheila?"

"I'm being as honest as I can right now," Sheila stated in short tones. "Please stop picking at my brain and trying to cross-examine me like I was a wayward teenager, Hannah. I need you to be my friend, not a jailer."

"Certainly." The housekeeper was unperturbed. Sheila only showed her temper when she was upset and afraid, and not yet ready to talk about it. If left alone, she would eventually apologize and then share her feelings. Hannah had learned a lot about her charge over the last months, and she knew that there was not a malicious bone in Sheila's body. But what had happened at the cabin?

They drove the rest of the way in virtual silence, with Hannah commenting every so often on the scenery, or sharing a brief tidbit of local goings-on. Sheila listened, but seldom replied beyond polite monosyllables. She was confused, and at some deep subconscious level, even more frightened than ever. She had a feeling that her life was about to change dramatically—again—and she still wasn't sure of her ability to cope, with any amount of grace and serenity.

She spent the next few days doing the artwork for the verses she had completed at the cabin. The one for a child's birthday was her favorite: she had surrounded the verse on the inside, as well as the cover, with delicate drawings of all the flowers she had found at the cabin, and 'Happy Birthday' cleverly woven in between the petals and leaves. After she finished it she sat for many minutes staring at it, remembering that it was one of the ones she had had such a hard time capturing. That had been the day Cole had first appeared at the door, and had asked her what she did for a living. It was also the first time he had held her, and she had reacted like an absolute ninny. What was the matter with her anyway? Why couldn't she react to him with the same easy wit and charm as she did all the other men she had known and dated over the years? *O, Lord*, she prayed silently, desperately, *when are You going to show me the way out of the valley? Why do I keep getting more and more confused? Why can't I forget Cole Hampton?*

Helping Hannah do the laundry and clean the house kept her occupied the day after she finished the artwork. After supper she wandered outside in the backyard to enjoy the cool evening, and was watering the daffodils and hyacinths on the back fence when Hannah called to her from the back steps.

"Sheila! There's someone here to see you!" There was a note in her voice that sent a spasm of alarm zig-zagging down Sheila's spine. Hannah sounded shaken. Who could it be? Could it be? Was it?

It was. He was standing in their living room, studying the collection of photographs depicting Sheila at every stage of her life, including the one taken just before her parents had been killed. Sheila never looked at that one—that portrayed a smiling, carefree girl who thought God had granted her every blessing in the book. How little she had known then! How much she had needed to grow. The painful character analysis was cut short when Cole turned, and the ice in the gray gaze froze her where she stood.

"At least you had the courtesy to leave a note this time." He put his hand into the inner pocket of the light ultra suede jacket he was wearing and drew out her note. "'I'm leaving so you won't have to feel obligated to play seeing-eye dog any more.'" He read the words with a deliberate lack of emphasis, his voice pronouncing them with cutting clarity. "You know what you are, Sheila Jamison? You're a coward."

Up went her chin. "You haven't changed, I see. You're still as rude, arrogant and overbearing as ever." She gave him look for look, but she was unused to this kind of verbal warfare and her heart wasn't in it. It never had been. Long lashes swept down to screen the sudden brightness in her eyes, and her hands dragged nervously through her hair.

"Sheila? Mr. Hampton?" Hannah had appeared in the doorway, her own frowning gaze taking in the two tense figures, though the imposing man looked more threatening than tense. "Can I offer you some iced tea or a Coke? And I made a cobbler for dessert—there's plenty left."

Cole's eyes swung to the hovering figure of the housekeeper. "Not right now, thank you. I'd just like to talk to Sheila. We were about to go for a drive in my car."

"Hmph," Hannah shook her head, watching the way Sheila had started at Mr. Hampton's announcement and not liking it one bit. "Sheila, you better get a sweater, then. The evenings are still cool."

A tide of color rose almost painfully as Sheila confronted his infernal stubborness once more. It was dreadfully awkward, however, with Hannah looking like a fat mother hen readying to attack the hungry fox. "I—I'd rather not," she risked a quick look at Cole from beneath her lashes. "Could we just sit here, maybe?" Now she turned to Hannah with a look that spoke volumes. "Hannah usually walks across the street after supper to visit with our neighbors, and I know it would relieve her mind if someone was here with me."

Cole didn't answer for a minute. His eyes swept over her slender figure, seeming to see behind the facade of control straight into her turbulent and confused mind. The harshness faded somewhat from his face, and his body lost some of its intimidating toughness. "All right. That's fine with me." He marked Hannah with a half-amused, half-irritated look. "Go visit your friends. I'm not going to harm the girl, or do anything that you couldn't share with the ladies at church."

"Hmph," Hannah said again. She wiped her hands on the tattered apron that covered her ample frame and then reached behind to untie the strings. "I'll be going then. Sheila, you make sure you give him some of that cobbler."

After she had left there was a small silence, then Cole moved to sink easily down to an overstuffed chair. It needed to be re-upholstered, but Sheila had never had the heart to cover it in a new fabric.

"That was always Daddy's favorite chair," she remarked now, feeling an unwelcome shyness hampering her tongue. "He used to sit there every evening after supper and read the paper."

"Both your parents are dead, I believe you told me."

She nodded. "They died within six months of each other."

He sat forward, clasping his hands loosely as he propped them on his knees. "My parents both died in a plane crash. I was seventeen, and for a long time I really let it control me—dropped out of school, kicked around at odd jobs until the mood struck to move on." He leaned back then, closed his eyes. "Then I joined the Marines to keep from getting drafted and ended up in Vietnam anyway." His eyes opened suddenly and zeroed in on Sheila. "You find out a lot about yourself in conditions like that, Sheila. And I found out, since life has no guarantees and you only get one shot at it, that I'd rather spend my time controlling things instead of letting them control me."

"You've been through a lot more than I have, I know," Sheila had sat down on the couch, and her fingers idly traced the patterns of blue and gray stripes. "and I've already told you—on several different occasions—that I realize I'm not handling my situation very well. So if all you came here to do was deliver another lecture, I'd just as soon forego the privilege. I get quite enough lectures from Hannah and Doris."

"Then why don't you listen?"

Sheila shot to her feet, the lines of her body taut as her eyes caught fire. "I'm trying!" she exclaimed furiously, hands clenched in tight fists at her sides. "Don't you think I'd give anything to just laugh it off and go my merry way and not worry any more? Not wonder? Doubt? Be afraid?" She shifted her gaze to the photograph behind Cole. "You'd like that Sheila back—the one who thought life was one glorious day after another? Well, so would I. But she's dead—as dead as if the man in the car had killed her, and nothing you or anyone can say is going to bring her back. So it—"

"Shut up!" he snapped with such ferocity that she backed up a step, her own anger fizzling out like a carbonated drink gone flat. "I don't ever want to hear you talk like that again, do you hear?'' He reached her in two giant strides and clamped her shoulders with a grip that was just short of brutal. "I can't abide self-pitying people, Sheila, and right now you reek of it. So you've got a handicap—it could be worse—but there are thousands of other handicapped people, who don't sit around feeling sorry for themselves. They do what they can with what they've got, and I expect you to do the same." The gray eyes lashed her, and he administered a brief shake before he let her go and strode angrily toward the front door. "Forget it. I thought you might be worth my time, but I've changed my mind." The door slammed behind him, and Sheila sank slowly back onto the sofa as tears rolled down her burning cheeks.

Everything he said was true, but nobody had said it quite so openly before. In fact, everyone had gone out of his way to smooth her path, cushion the blow life had handed her. She had been petted, cosseted, treated like a helpless baby for so long that she was beginning to think she *was* helpless. No . . . she knew better, but it had been easier to give in than to do what she should have done months ago: face reality and deal with it. She was sitting on the couch, face buried in her hands as tears burned slowly down and trickled through her fingers, when Hannah came charging through the door.

"What happened, honey? I saw Mr. Hampton tearing off down the street like a moonshiner with the sheriff on his heels." She stared at Sheila's flushed face with concern. "Did that man hurt you? Oh, I knew I should have stayed here. All those stories about him are true, aren't they? What happened? I'll go call Joe—I'm not going to have anyone—"

"Hannah, please don't." she lifted her head, swiped at the tears with the back of her hand and then took a deep, tremulous breath. "I deserved it." Without further explanation she rose and moved like an old, weary woman out of the living room and down the hall to her bedroom. Right now it would take too much of an effort to attempt an explanation.

"I'm going for a walk," she announced the next morning after breakfast. She stared the housekeeper down, her eyes black with the determination and inner turmoil. "Don't worry. I'll be all right, and if I go blind—" she used the words deliberately, eschewing the phrase she normally used, *have a spell,* "—I'll just ask someone to guide me to the nearest phone, or bring me home."

Hannah started to say something, looked into Sheila's face again and changed her mind. Drawing a deep breath, she smoothed her work-roughened hands over her ample lap. "Very well," she yielded reluctantly.

The town of Camden had installed sidewalks in this neighborhood some fifteen years before, and Sheila strolled toward the main section of town now with a mixture of fear and exhilaration dogging her footsteps. It had been easier than she had expected, mainly because Hannah had not put up the fuss Sheila had anticipated. Her head twisted suddenly in suspicion to gaze behind her, but she saw nothing save the Oates' tomcat Oliver lounging in the morning sun. She had stopped to scratch his ears, smiling at the rumbling purr that resulted as the animal stretched lazily and stropped himself against her legs before flopping onto his back to enjoy her ministrations. It would be nice to be a cat. That brought to mind thoughts of Cole Hampton, and Sheila had continued walking with firm steps, though her heart was pounding and her palms were cold and clammy despite the balmy weather.

She made it to the post office three blocks away before running into somebody and receiving her first lecture. Birdie Bates had been postmistress of Camden for thirty-one years and knew as much about the residents as Doc Farmer, who at one time had been Camden's only physician before the town mushroomed right after the war.

"What are you doing so far from home alone, young lady?" Birdie called through the open door of the post office. Her voice, as chipper as a bird's, and her diminutive stature had earned her her nickname years ago.

"I'm going for a walk," Sheila smiled in patient resignation. "Yes, I'm alone, and yes, I know it's taking a chance, and no, I don't want any help."

"Hannah giving you a hard time?" Birdie ventured shrewdly. She walked down the brick steps, her brook brown eyes twinkling merrily.

"She was really very restrained," Sheila supplied, a grin tugging at her lips, "but the air was thick with her thoughts."

"Well, I'm pleased you're venturing out a little more. It's good for you." She gave Sheila a smug smile and turned to climb back up the steps. "Just yell out if you need help and I'm within hearing range."

Well, that hadn't been as bad as she thought it would be either, which was probably an omen, or at the very least a sign. She would do well to heed it and maybe, just maybe she could widen the parameters of her cage. Drat Cole anyway. Why did he always have to be right? And why did it hurt so badly when she had to face the fact that she would probably never see him again?

As she strolled along, her steps gradually slowed as her thoughts grew more and more dismal. He had been so angry yesterday, almost frightening, and his parting words had burned into her heart like a brand. She would never forget them, nor the look of utter contempt that had been on his face. Something inside her twisted in a spasm of pain, and she realized with a sense of shock that she was hurting with the same kind of hurt that had descended when she had first found out about her vision. And it was then, while she was standing in a frozen vacuum that precluded the rest of the world, that she realized she had fallen in love with Cole Hampton.

Love was supposed to make the sky bluer, the grass greener, the world rosier than ever. Flowers were supposed to smell sweeter, and the birdsong should have the crystalline clarity of a heavenly choir. Her heart . . . her heart was supposed to be joyful. But she was oblivious to the sights and sounds, and her heart beat a throbbing rhythm of pain that echoed down interminable years of barrenness. She turned blindly, jerkily, to retrace her steps, uncaring of any new freedoms that she might have gained, and all because of Cole.

"Sheila! Hey, Sheila? What on earth are you doing, child?" Mr. Porter hailed her from across the street. He had been pruning his marigolds, but was now standing there with astonishment and concern plain in his lined face.

Sheila looked neither to right nor left before she stepped off the curb, her natural courtesy rising above the agony to prevent her from ignoring the kindly old widower whose only pleasure in life now was his flowers. He and her mother used to have a friendly but fierce competition to see who could produce the most spectacular garden each spring. . . .

"Sheila—watch out!"

The piercing blast of a horn and the ear-splitting screech of brakes shattered the morning as well as Sheila's catatonic trance. She jumped back instinctively, her eyes black with shock as a car managed to halt mere inches from her body.

"Sheila, are you all right?" Mr. Porter was beside her, patting her hands, and then the driver of the car was there, yelling at her.

"Why didn't you look where you were going?" It was a man—another angry man, some distant portion of Sheila registered with fleeting humor—and his face was doubtless as ashen as her own.

"I'm sorry," she managed to apologize, her gaze encompassing both men. "I—I wasn't thinking. . . ."

"I shouldn't have called out to you like that," interjected Mr. Porter, his own voice sounding shaken.

"Well, you're lucky I could stop!" snapped the driver as he climbed back into his car.

Sheila allowed Mr. Porter to help her back across the street, and they both watched as the car gunned away. "You think he'd at least slow down," Sheila commented absently. She pressed trembling fingers over her eyes, then turned to her elderly friend. "Are you all right, Mr. Porter? I guess I gave you a pretty bad shock, didn't I?"

"Not as bad as the one you got, I imagine," he replied with returning good humor. "Though I confess you managed to squeeze a few more beats out of the old ticker than it's used to." He frowned at her. "What are you doing down this far by yourself, Sheila? You usually stick to your own yard when you're alone."

"I will in the future, too," Sheila muttered, only now fully comprehending how close she had come to another, probably more devastating tragedy. Cole was wrong. She had just proved that she couldn't be trusted off a short leash, and if the driver of that car hadn't had good reflexes. . . .

"Next time you want to compare gardens, give me a whistle," Mr. Porter patted her shoulder again. "I'd be glad to escort you. But maybe you better be a little more careful in the future to keep your eyes open, hmm? Especially at these times when you've got two good ones."

"Thanks, Mr. Porter. And I'm sorry about giving you such a jolt. But it's nothing like the jolt my heart has had, and I don't think I'll ever recover.

Sheila called Doris that evening. They hadn't really had a chance to talk since the Allendres' return from their Caribbean trip, and it was on this pretext that Sheila invited her friend over for a chat.

" . . . and now that I've spent the last thirty minutes rhapsodizing over our vacation, I suppose I better hush so you can tell me how you've been." Doris scrutinized the younger woman, and a small frown gathered between her brows. "Something's the matter, isn't it? You didn't ask me over to hear about the trip. Come on, Sheila. Talk. What's wrong?"

"So much that I don't really know where to begin." Sheila laughed, a travesty of a laugh that didn't fool Doris for one minute. "I didn't want to dump on you like this, but I honestly don't know what to do or who else to go to. Hannah mothers me and worries herself to death, and Elaine throws activities at me like bullets to keep me diverted . . . and I just don't know what to do." Her voice died away into a pool of silence, then Doris prodded very calmly, very quietly.

"So tell me about it. Things are never as bad as they seem, you know, even for you."

" 'Even for me,' " Sheila echoed, and her mouth twisted. "Doris, what would you say if I told you I had met a man and fallen in love?"

There was another short silence. "I'd say that was marvelous," Doris replied at last, her voice carefully neutral. "Who is it, and when did it happen? Obviously while we were gone, but that was only three weeks. Are you sure it's love?"

"I've never felt this way before, if that's what you mean. I suppose it could be infatuation, and to be brutally honest, I hope that's all there is to it."

"Why, honey?"

"Because the love—or infatuation—most definitely is not mutual." Sheila stated flatly.

Doris winced. "Oh, dear, are you sure? Who is it, anyway? Somebody I know? Is he from church?"

Sheila took a deep breath, looked down at her fingers and noticed that they were trembling. A wry smile just touched the corners of her mouth as she looked back up at Doris. "You know him, but he's not from church." Keeping her gaze steady, she revealed with quiet resignation, "It's Cole, Doris. I think I'm in love with Cole Hampton."

"Dear God in heaven," Doris said, and her eyes closed briefly. When she opened them it was obvious that she was still shaken. "When did this happen, Sheila? How?"

"I went up to Elaine's parents' cabin last a week. Cole has a summer home on the same lake. We met, and in spite of his behavior, I fell in love with him."

"What do you mean 'in spite of his behavior?' What did he do?"

"Now you sound like Hannah." Sheila smiled briefly. "He didn't do anything except treat me like a person instead of an invalid, and most of the time as an *unwanted* person. It's not his fault I'm a desperate spinster of hopeless means just waiting for a man to smile once so I can fall at his feet."

"Sheila, you're avoiding the issue as well as being maddeningly vague. If you want advice or opinions from me, you're going to have to do better, especially when it concerns Cole Hampton." She studied Sheila, and there was something in the quality of that measuring perusal that caused Sheila to stir uneasily. "You forget I've known him a lot longer than you have, and while I realize a lot of what we hear is unfounded gossip, a lot of it is *well* founded and anything but gossip." She paused. "Cole is not the kind of man you need to be involved with, honey. I hate to have to say that, but it usually causes nothing but heartache when a dedicated Christian tries to force a relationship with a non-Christian."

"Doris, I didn't try to force anything. It just *happened*." Her voice was desperate now. "I didn't

96

want to feel this way! I wanted to fall in love with a Christian man and marry and have children and bring them up in the way they should go and live happily ever after. It doesn't always work out like that, though." Her voice dropped, and she finished in a dull monotone. "Lots of things in life don't work like you want. . . ."

"If that's how you've felt about life, then I think maybe all that has happened to you might be necessary." Doris' voice was tart, and though her eyes were warm, her expression was stern. "Just because you're one of God's children doesn't mean He's going to give you everything you *want*, Sheila. He promised to supply all our *needs*, and to give us the grace and strength to face whatever life throws at us, good or bad. You've been very fortunate to have been tossed so much good before the bad. That should give you *more* strength, not *less*." She help up her hand as Sheila started to speak. "Let me finish. Joe and I have been watching you all these months, and we know you're going through the 'dark night of the soul,' I believe someone once called it. Okay, you have a lot of questions, a lot of things you don't understand. But that doesn't mean you need to turn your back on your faith and run as hard as you can the other way."

"I knew you were going to say that." Sheila sighed. "All right. I'll try to explain so you won't have the wrong idea and start panicking because I'm about to renounce my Christianity and my chastity all at the same time." She glanced at her watch. "Hannah should be coming home in about an hour. Promise me—*promise me*, Doris, that you won't ever breathe a word of this to her. She worries, you know, even when she doesn't say anything, and I just couldn't bear to hurt her or give her more cause to worry." Or more cause to suffocate me, she added silently. "The first time I met Cole I made a fool of myself, remember?"

"I remember."

There it was again, that indefinable tone of voice that sent tiny little trickles of unease snaking down her spine. She shook off the feeling and continued. "I never expected to see him again—part of me hoped I never would see him again. But even way back, then another part of me couldn't forget him." She looked down at her laced fingers. "I suppose I'm no different from any other woman. He even told me—" she paused, and blushed.

"You may as well say it," Doris' voice was resigned. "I don't think you can shock me anymore than you have already."

"He told me he wanted to have an affair after meeting me that first time," Sheila blurted out, the blush deepening. "But then I had that accident. . . ."

"Yes, the accident." Her voice was so peculiar, and the look on her face suddenly guarded.

Sheila didn't notice. She was too caught up in releasing some of her intolerable burden and the words spilled forth, almost tumbling over themselves. "He didn't recognize me at the cabin, and of course at first I didn't recognize him, either. Anyway, he flat out told me he was up there to be alone and he didn't want anything to do with women. But when he found out who I was—well, Doris, he started chasing me. Yes, *chasing* me. Of course that was after I fell into the lake because I went blind and had gone for a walk by myself like a ninny, and Cole rescued me. Then he knew about my attacks of blindness, so I didn't know if he was interested because of me or because he felt sorry for me." She put her hands over her eyes, then ran them agitatedly through her hair. "I still didn't know when I came home and then when he came to see me the other day, I was such a wretched little dip. . .and so he got mad and left—and I know I'll never see him again." Her incoherent rambling stopped, and her voice dropped to a whisper, as she shook her head in agonized bewilderment. "But he was so gentle with me—so kind. Why? I just don't understand—and I can't help what I feel. I just can't help it. He didn't try anything—nothing. And I didn't want to feel this way, but I do. I do. Doris . . . I begged God to make these feelings go away, to help me understand. I—"

"Sheila, slow down. Wait a minute, now, and let me sort through what you've said. You say Cole knows about your attacks of blindness?"

Sheila nodded.

"What was his reaction?"

She pondered that a minute, and a look of wonderment filled her face. "He was upset. He really was— only I was too scared at the time to realize it. Doris, he wasn't disgusted or anything. He was upset, I'd even say concerned for me. . . ."

Doris didn't say anything, but the frown on her face deepened.

"But that's also the reason I'll never see him again," Sheila continued after a minute, and the look of wonder faded to the white, pinched look that had alarmed Doris when Sheila had first opened the door earlier. "He told me I was a coward, and that he hated self-pitying people like me, then he walked out." She forced herself to say the words matter-of-factly, but it was an effort.

"Why did he call you such—um, unflattering names?" Doris asked then, the merest glimmer of a smile pepping through the frowning concern.

"Well . . . I more or less ran out on him at the lake, and then when he came to see me, I said—" She turned her head aside, eaten with shame at the memory of those emotional words she had flung so carelessly. "I said I couldn't be the Sheila I used to be and that the man who had hit me had killed her." She turned back as Doris gasped, and the sense of shame deepened. "It was unforgivable, I know, and I don't

99

blame him for walking out. Nobody cares for shrewish women, and I'm not exactly anyone's idea of the ideal woman at the moment.''

''Sheila. . . .'' She seemed at a loss for words, and Sheila watched her, feeling that trickle of unease widening to a fast-running stream.

''What's the matter, Doris? Has Cole said something to Joe? Is it me?''

''No . . . I'm just at a loss for words.'' Doris searched her mind, deliberating over the choice of her next words. ''Sheila, I will say this. I don't pretend to know or understand everything about Cole Hampton, but I do know *you* pretty well. I've noticed over the last few years that you have this tendency to model yourself after some manufactured ideal of what you consider to be the 'perfect Christian woman.' I think that's partly why you've had such a hard time adjusting to your handicap—you're condemning yourself because you're not perfect. And I think in some deep part of you, that you're blaming Cole because you think he wants the perfect woman you used to be. Now, like I said, I don't claim to know everything about Cole, but if he told you he was. . .uh. . .attracted to you from the first time he met you, then it's probably true. Cole Hampton is a straightforward man, and honest, even if he's not a Christian. Now you say he's changed his mind.'' She looked over at Sheila, waiting. Sheila nodded. ''Well, my dear, for your sake I hope you're right. But something deep inside of me says that that's not the way it is at all.'' She stood, and wrapped a comforting arm around the younger woman almost as if she were keeping at bay all the nefarious Cole Hampton's of the world who sought to harm her in any way. ''I think you're wrong. I don't think you've seen the last of Cole Hampton at all.''

CHAPTER 6

SHE WAS HANGING OUT LAUNDRY when it happened next. She reached into the clothes basket for another sheet and the blackness descended with the ruthlessness of a machete. Sheila tried to make it back to the house without calling Hannah, in the process tripping over the first porch step and falling, bruising her cheek and skinning both hands and a knee. Hannah patched her up, anguish clouded her plump face even as she refrained from voicing any remonstrations.

Sheila spent the next two days clambering around the house and yard, refusing any and all aid. She lurched into furniture, spilled food and drink, and in her total despair reverted to almost total withdrawal. She would never be independent, never be able to function with skill and grace when she was blind, never be able to douse the coals of fire heaped upon her head by Cole Hampton.

On the third day of darkness she finally yielded to her frayed nerves and yelled at Hannah, ordering her out of the house. "Just leave me alone!" she sobbed, arms hugging her sides as the emotion tore through her body. "Go away and leave me alone. I'm tired of pretending I can manage when I can't!"

"I'll be across the street. Call when you want me to come home." Hannah hesitated, wanting to take Sheila in her arms so desperately that tears clouded her eyes as well. Wiping them on her apron, she lumbered sadly out the front door and across the street.

Sheila stumbled over the edge of the carpet and fell, then crawled her way over to the sofa where she collapsed, body heaving as the tears racked through her. She never heard the knock on the door, or the firm steps that covered the distance to her side. When a hand touched her hair lightly, then pushed a damp curl off her forehead, she didn't even respond.

"Sheila," Cole's voice was as unexpected as her ridiculous notion of an appearance by the angel Gabriel, and she was so startled that she lifted her head to stare blindly in the direction of that voice. She heard the hiss of his indrawn breath, and then strong, infinitely tender arms came around her, held her close. "Shh, baby, please don't cry," he murmured against her hair, and her heart twisted in a spasm of fresh grief at that soft note of tenderness. She did love him, she did, and she would never have the comfort of that voice, those arms for her very own, for always.

"Sheila," he whispered again, and his hands wiped away the tears, traced gently over the wet, sightless eyes and soft, quivering mouth. "Don't do this to yourself, honey. You're killing me."

"Cole?" Her voice was hoarse, almost a croak, and her own hands lifted slowly, tentatively, finding his face and feeling for herself that he was really here. "Why are you here? You hate me, you never—"

"Hush." He placed a finger over her lips. "You made me angry, sweetheart. I didn't really mean what I said, and you should have known it." Not for worlds would he admit that at the time he *had* meant it, that he had meant to cut her out of his life and not look back, because he knew in his gut that Sheila Jamison was dangerous. But when Joe had confided this morning that she had been blind now for three days, and that he and Doris were worried about her, Cole had found himself totally unable to let it go. It was his fault, *his* fault, and he had cursed steadily and fluently through the interminable day, until even his unflappable secretary had covered the typewriter and walked out on him.

Unable to function and unable to confide in the Allendres, he had come to Sheila, ready to exorcise her once and for all, and now found the stranglehold tighter than ever. Maybe if he went ahead and confessed . . . she would probably hate *him*, then, and tell him to get out of her life. Maybe then he could get on with the rest of *his* life. But the thought of her looking at him with those incredible eyes full of hatred and recriminations was even more unthinkable now than it had been nine months ago. He couldn't do it, God help him. The ruthless, take-control-of-all-circumstances-and-do-it-my-way Cole Hampton had been reduced by five-feet-four-inches of feminine floss who was totally unaware of her power.

"I don't hate you, little one, though I do hate to see you like this." He touched her eyes again, his touch as light as thistledown. "Joe said it's been three days now. Are you that scared, honey?" Now his searching fingers were moving over the bruised cheek, and then he was lifting her chin. "Sheila. Talk to me, there's a good girl."

Later she consoled herself that even a stone statue would have crumbled at the gentleness in that voice, so there was no reason for her to be ashamed of her actions. And she tried, she had tried to control her voice, to stem the tears and discuss her feelings with dignity and maturity. But he was too perceptive, too able to pry loose all her defenses.

"Oh, Cole . . . I tried so hard!" She choked back one sob. "I tried to be capable, su–sufficient like other ha–handicapped people, but I just couldn't do it!" This time the sob escaped, and then she collapsed against his chest, crying out the rest of the fear and pain and hopelessness of all the last long months.

Cole let her cry, settling himself on the sofa and hauling her onto his lap, stroking gentle fingers through her tumbled hair. He had known a lot of women who could cry on command and whose tears were about as sincere as the crocodile's; never had he seen a woman cry with the utter abandon and disregard for the damage she was doing to her looks he was seeing in Sheila now. He felt helpless and guilty, but he also felt an alien compassion so strong that it overpowered everything else. He sensed that this vulnerable woman needed him right now more than he had ever been needed in his life, and he had to respond.

She regained control at last, and the sobs gradually quieted to shuddering whimpers. Then there was silence as she lay heavily against him, her hands clutching almost desperately to the now damp collar of his shirt.

"I'm sorry," she managed to choke out in a tiny voice, keeping her head buried in his shoulder. "You shouldn't have come here when I was like this."

His hand tugged gently on the curls at the nape of her neck, and she was forced to reveal the ravaged, tear-soaked face. "But that's precisely why I'm here," he told her gently, and an handkerchief began mopping up the damage. "You needed someone—I like to think you needed me. How long have you kept this bottled up inside, anyway?"

Sheila ignored the faint stirring remnants of pride and blew her nose while he held the handkerchief for her. "Nine months," she confessed sheepishly. "This is the longest I've ever been blind, and I guess it all had to come out." She tried to move off his lap, but Cole merely tightened his grip.

"Just stay where you are," he commanded with teasing humor. Then his manner changed, resumed a serious tone. "Are you still afraid, honey?"

Not with you here, Sheila wanted to admit. But she knew that she would go to her grave before she would reveal her true feelings to him. "A little, but not as much as before. Psychologists do maintain that a good cry does wonders for the psyche."

"Then yours ought to be in tip-top shape. Ah-ah, don't go all defensive on me, I was only teasing." He lifted her hand and dropped a brief kiss on her moist palm, laughing softly as she jerked. "You told me once that there was one doctor who had mentioned the possibility of an operation. Have you considered it?"

The question was asked so casually that, for a minute, Sheila was lulled by the timbre of his voice before the import of his words struck. She gave a strangled, bitter laugh and touched her hand to her eyes. "Oh, yes, I *considered* it! I considered being permanently blind or being turned into a vegetable or being paralyzed . . . maybe all of the above."

"Are those probable risks as told to you by the doctor, or just what you're afraid might happen?"

"Those were the probable risks, as outlined in vivid detail by *all* the doctors. Don't you think I was grasping at straws, too? But they all agreed it was too big a risk, and the doctor from Duke said he's tried the procedure I would need only once before—unsuccessfully. Not a very good track record." She started as Cole's hands caught hers, dragging them down from where they had been rubbing her eyes.

"Take it easy, honey. We'll let it ride for now." She felt his fingers caressing hers, stroking tenderly the still raw surfaces on her palms. "Speaking of rides . . . Dr. Hampton prescribes a change of atmosphere for you." He stood, set her gently on her feet but kept a comforting hand on her shoulder. "Since this is your home I presume you know the way to your bathroom. Go wash your face and hands, and then put on some slacks." There was a definite thread of wicked laughter in the words now. "Not that I don't approve of these delightfully threadbare shorts, but I might decide to take us somewhere for a bite to eat after we drive around awhile." He ruffled her hair with what felt like teasing affection. "I presume you can also find your way to your own bedroom?"

Sheila responded with a rueful smile that faded almost immediately to a grimace. "The last couple of days I'm beginning to wonder." She stopped as she realized that she was about to bemoan her clumsiness again, and that it would sound like she was feeling sorry for herself. She had already acted such a fool in front of him that she should be grateful, whatever the reason for Cole's unexplained appearance—even if it was only pity.

"You've been fighting it the last couple of days." He turned her gently around. "Now I want you to use your brain and relax. I'll give you twenty minutes— show me you can beat a woman who is able to see herself in the mirror and thus waste twice that time."

She presented herself again twenty-three minutes later, standing awkwardly in the entrance to the living room while she waited for Cole to comment. "Do I match?" she asked at last, and forced a self-depreciating laugh. "Are my eyes and nose still all red and puffy. . . ?"

"Your clothes match just fine, and yes, your eyes and nose are still a designer shade of red, but I'll take you along, anyway. Sheila. . . ."

His voice was abrupt, almost clipped, and Sheila froze inside. "Yes?" she waited, not moving, her heart fluttering like bird wings.

"Are you afraid of riding in a car?"

106

"No . . . just a little nervous. I've had to do it several times, so it's getting easier." She hesitated, then offered as casually as she could, "If you'd rather not, I understand. It doesn't matter, Cole."

He muttered something under his breath, then his hand clamped around her forearm in a far from gentle grip. "Let's go, then. Do you need to leave a note for your amazon of a housekeeper?"

"Yes," she faltered, and turned toward the little table in the hall where she knew there was a pen and pad by the phone. Cole's hand restrained her.

"Here," he said, and she heard him ripping a piece of paper. He watched without comment as she took the pen he gave her and managed to write a legible note without going off the edge. Then he propelled her without further comment outside and into his car.

She could tell it was fairly large and probably more than fairly expensive. The seats were a soft, supple leather and as cushioned as an easy chair. They rode for a few minutes in silence, and Sheila found that it was not hard to relax after all. Cole had turned the radio to a station with unobtrusive easy listening music that poured over her taut nerves like a bath of warm oil. "Is that the station you usually listen to?" she asked eventually, and Cole chuckled.

"Nope. But I figured it was the kind of thing you'd probably prefer. Am I right?"

"Actually, I go in strictly for classical music." Sheila intoned in her most affected, pious accent, and then felt a sense of wonder that she was actually teasing Cole as she might have done a year ago.

"Well in that case . . . " She could hear him fiddling with the dials, and suddenly discordant strains of some modern composer rent the air.

Sheila covered her ears. "I should have said C and W."

"There's plenty of that around here," Cole grinned. His hand covered hers, and its warmth and strength were as potent as the final strains of Handel's "Hallelujah Chorus" from the *Messiah*. "It's good to see you like this, Sheila. YOu don't know how——" He bit off whatever he had been going to say, and after a minute removed his hand.

Sheila turned her head so that she knew he could see her face if he chose. "Cole, why did you come?" she pressed quietly. "Is it because you feel sorry for me?"

"Partly," he answered curtly.

Sheila flinched, but it was no more than she had expected. She hadn't expected the truth to cut so deeply, however, and she turned her head toward the window, not wanting him to see how much he had hurt her.

"I said *partly*," Cole emphasized with grating coolness. "You know the other reason, if you're brave enough to admit it."

"I thought——you haven't——oh." She was as helplessly flustered as a schoolgirl, and Cole's soft, taunting laughter only served to further disconcert her. "But I'm blind!" she burst out, then clapped her hands over her mouth as she waited for his blistering attack.

"What the——what does that have to do with it?" There was no expression in the quiet voice, so Sheila was unable to tell whether or not he was angry.

She waited, scarcely daring to breath, and after a minute she heard him expel his breath in an explosive sigh that mingled frustration, irritation, and regret. "Sheila, if you could see right now it would make this a lot easier, but the fact that you're blind does not lessen my desire for you one iota. You were a lovely woman when I met you last summer, and——in spite of the changes——you are still a lovely woman. But . . . " his words trailed away again, almost as if he regretted having said them, and Sheila could no longer endure the silence.

"But it's hard to desire a woman you feel sorry for, isn't it?" she finished for his, and gasped when the car swerved suddenly and jerked to a stop.

"That's not what it is at all," Cole gritted from between clenched teeth.

Sheila heard the sound of movement and then his door opened and slammed with a force that jarred her teeth. She had just enough time to wonder if he had left her when her door opened and his hands unfastened her seatbelt with rough impatience. Then he lifted her out and stood her beside him, keeping his hands clamped around her arms like handcuffs. "Wouldn't you like to know where we are?"

There was such an ominous note in the heavily spoken words that Sheila felt a tremor start deep inside. Cole must have felt it, too, for he abruptly pulled her close and held her for a minute, then just as abruptly put her from him. Sheila raised both arms to rub her elbows.

"Where are we?" she asked, licking suddenly dry lips and feeling the oppressive black veil closing in around her and trying to choke her breath as well as her sight.

"We're about a mile from my house," Cole stated in a flat, harsh tone that scraped across her quivering nerves. "Right where you had your accident, to be exact. Where 'that man—killed you,' I believe was how you put it?"

"What is it, Cole? Why are you talking like that?" She was almost afraid, and totally bewildered. He sounded like a man in agony, and perhaps because she could not see, the emotion in his voice was that much more intensified to her. A thought flashed into her brain like a blinking yellow warning light. "Are you trying to make me face my past—is that it?"

"No." The single syllable was tortured, and then she was being hauled into a violent embrace. His mouth came down on hers, and he kissed her with a

109

forcefulness and desperation that brought tears stinging to the surface. Too bewildered to struggle, she submitted limply, some part of her registering that even now, when he wasn't trying to be loving or tender at all, her body was still responding, still bursting into aching life at his touch.

His mouth finally lifted, and a soft but explicit curse caused her to flinch. He apologized immediately, and then pressed her head hard against his shoulder. "Sheila . . . I've got to tell you!—" He was speaking over her head now, still in that tortured voice that was reflected in the rigidity of the arms that held her so close. "Your accident—your blindness . . . it's my fault." She felt him suck in his breath as if it hurt his lungs. "I was the man driving the other car that night. I was the man who swerved to avoid hitting those people and hit you instead. Oh, God!" he groaned, "why couldn't I have rammed a tree? Why did it have to be you?"

At first she was so stunned she couldn't move, couldn't think. *Cole? Cole* who had caused this awful, unbearable burden? Then, as if the clouds were rolled back to reveal a pure white light illuminating her mind, it hit her that Cole was blaming himself. Not only blaming himself, but allowing the guilt to eat him as she was allowing the fear to nibble her up a bite at the time. And it was Cole who had suffered painful injuries, injuries that were really more painful than her own had been. Concussions, she knew, could be dangerous. And he had broken several bones . . . and here he was agonizing over what he had done to her.

She lifted her arms, her hands finding his face, her fingers caressing the taut bones and beard-roughened flesh. "Cole," she murmured urgently. "Cole, don't do this to yourself. Listen to me, Cole. It's all right— nobody was at fault. I was wrong to feel the way I did. Cole . . . ?"

Now it was his hands that framed her face, and

even though she couldn't see, Sheila knew his eyes were burning into hers with that intent scrutiny she remembered so well. She didn't even try to mask her feelings at that moment. Cole's feelings were all that mattered, and the wounds to his own soul were the ones that needed healing now.

"Sheila," he whispered in unsteady accents, "you're not angry—"

She shook her head vigorously. "Of course not! You chose the only available option, and you only had a fraction of a second to make that choice. You *would* have killed that couple had you struck them, but I had the protection of my car, so you did the only thing you could have done." She smiled slightly. "Now I probably would have panicked and killed everybody!"

"But I caused you to be blind—to cut your beautiful hair. I ruined your life."

She listened to him repeat feelings she had wrestled with for all those months and felt a surge of repentance and shame so strong that she shook with it. So that was what she had sounded like . . . "Cole," she pursued now with a sincerity he couldn't doubt, "I don't blame you. In spite of what I said the other night when I was upset, you must believe me. I really don't blame you." She smiled again, a real smile. Haven't you ever lost your temper and said something you didn't mean? that was nothing but sheer frustration and pig-headedness. I know—have known deep inside—that no one was at fault last year. The problem I'm having to cope with now is not what you did. It's what I did to myself. Cole, please stop feeling guilty. Please."

There was dawning wonder in his voice when next he spoke, and an incredulous but growing relief. "You're unbelievable, did you know that? You're standing here looking up at me with you eyes so wide and guileless that even I can tell you're not lying to make me feel better. Such big, beautiful brown eyes that let me see all the way into your innocent little heart . . . and yet you can't see anything at all.'' His lips brushed across her lids in a salute so reverent, so gentle that the flame burning inside her deepened to white intensity. As his mouth moved slowly, softly across her forehead and down her cheek, her eyes fluttered shut and she melted into him, her arms sliding around his neck to hold him close.

''Such a sweet, forgiving mouth,'' he whispered against it, then his lips were nibbling all around the edges, until with a sigh she relaxed. With shattering tenderness so different from that other time, he kissed her, kissed her with a passion and warmth that offered an intimacy she had never known, never dreamed could exist. Her hands were clutching him, burrowing into the thickness of his hair, savoring the strength and solidity of him.

As if he were the one who was blind, Cole's hands began slowly tracing the contours of her face, stroking its softness. They found the pulse beating a frantic rhythm in her throat, and moved behind her head to tease the curls at the nape of her neck. When she suddenly gasped and pulled away, he released her gently. ''It's okay,'' he reassured her. ''I'm not going to hurt you.'' The ghost of a laugh wafted past her ears. ''I'm sorry. I didn't mean to frighten you—to get so carried away.''

''That's all right.'' Was that her voice, so breathless and unsure? She tried again, unobtrusively lowering her arms until they rested decorously on his chest. But she could feel his heart thundering beneath her fingertips, and when he laughed softly again, she knew that she was revealing the effect he had on her in a most unwise manner. ''I didn't mean to—to get carried away, either.''

His hands came up to cover hers, holding them in a firm clasp as he gently put a safer distance between them. "We'll just put it down to the emotion of the moment. He laughed a deep and unrestrained laugh. "Maybe we better go someplace nice and public before I corrupt my sweet little Christian any further." The laugh turned to a chuckle as Sheila tugged angrily at her trapped hands. "I'm not making fun of you, honey. I find you utterly delightful—even with your lack of experience."

"Oh!" The blush burned from her toes to her hairline. "If you don't stop trying to embarrass me, I'll—I'll—"

"You'll what?" he inquired with interest.

"I'll burn to death from blushing," she confessed, and grinned.

"Well, we certainly can't have that." He reached behind her to open the car door. "It would ruin all my plans for us." He pushed her gently inside, snapped her seatbelt back in place and shut the door. Sheila sat in dumb silence, his words reverberating back and forth in her head like the marble in a pinball machine.

"Have you eaten supper?" Cole asked as he slid in beside her and started the engine.

"Hannah cooked it, but I didn't eat anything." She sighed as memory of her behavior surfaced momentarily. "She tried to get me to eat and I'm afraid I wasn't very agreeable about it."

"I trust you'll be more so now. Hannah might not put you over her knee, but I would." He carefully reversed the car and they headed back in the other direction.

Sheila looked toward him, and wished that she could see his face. "Would you really?" she asked, curiosity and a smattering of uncertainty in her voice.

"No, you gullible little idiot. Can't you see—" he paused, then finished quietly, "I'm sorry. Of course you can't see that I'm joking."

No, but I can tell that you still feel guilty, Sheila wanted to say. She also wanted to weep, because she still didn't know why he was bothering with her. There were probably a dozen women within spitting distance who would jump through hoops to have Cole Hampton's attention, and who probably wouldn't have stopped at a kiss, either. There was no reason he should be taking her out, paying her attention . . . except for the guilt. Those passionate kisses had meant as much to him as a cold plate of scrambled eggs. If only she wasn't blind! Doris' words came to her, warning her about Cole and the pitfalls of a relationship with a man who didn't share her faith, and Sheila was forced to swallow another bitter dose of reality. She might as well enjoy his pity, because it was certain the relationship could go no further.

They ate in Roanoke at a restaurant casual enough for Sheila's poplin slacks and knit pullover, but cosmopolitan enough to keep Cole's business suit from looking out of place. Cole had quietly read the menu to her, and without fuss or awkwardness pointed out locations just as he had that evening in his lakeside home. Sheila found herself confessing quite candidly that this was her first experience at public dining while blind, and that he was making it so easy for her to relax. For the space of a couple of heartbeats he had been silent, then his hand squeezed hers briefly.

"Any time," he promised lightly, easing. "Someone should have taken you in hand months ago."

"I told you once that I don't need a seeing-eye dog." Sheila put her fork down very carefully. "Since the spells—the blind periods don't usually last this long, it's just easier to stay at home."

"Don't get defensive with me, Sheila," Cole responded, his voice deep and quiet. "I'm doing what I want to do with the person I want to do it with, and that's all there is to it. Quit looking for ulterior motives where there aren't any."

They spent the rest of the meal talking in a relaxed,

desultory fashion, largely because Sheila made a concerted effort to live for the moment and Cole made at least a half-hearted attempt to be charming and non-threatening. Sheila had a sneaking suspicion that, had he chosen to exert the full force of that charm, he could have had her dancing the flamenco on the tabletop with a rose between her teeth.

"What were you like when you were a little boy?" she asked him suddenly, halfway through dessert. Her piece of pie slid off the fork and Cole speared it with his own, then held it to her mouth before answering.

"I was probably an angel in my mother's eyes, but the truth is I was a little hellion. Real life 'Dennis the Menace'."

"Were you an only child, too?" Sheila could imagine him as a boy, covered with mud and climbing trees and riding his bike through fresh cement. . . .

"Not to begin with, no," he was replying, his voice musingly introspective. "I had an older brother, Mike. I used to bug the life out of him, always tailing along behind him and trying to do everything he did. Up to and including eating poison mushrooms when I was six and he was eight." Sheila gasped, knowing instinctively what was coming. "I only got sick, but Mike had a bad allergic reaction and died before any of us quite knew what was going on. It's funny . . . after almost thirty years I can still remember him as if it were yesterday."

"Oh, Cole." Her own voice catching, she reached blindly across the table in a spontaneous gesture of compassion—and knocked over her water glass. The tears that had been threatening to spill because of Cole's sad revelation welled up and over now due to humiliation.

Cole righted the glass and mopped up the moisture with his napkin without a word, then took her hand. "No one saw, honey. Don't look like that, either about the water or my brother. It was a long time ago

115

and I seldom think of it, much less talk about it." He squeezed her hand, insinuating his thumb underneath her clenched fingers and teasing them until they opened. "Give me a smile now, or I'll lean over and kiss you in front of everyone to take your mind off your misplaced sympathy."

"Could we go, please?" she pleaded in a subdued voice, and the smile she gave him was decidely wobbly at the edges.

She was withdrawn on the way home, unable to recapture her earlier mood. Cole didn't need the sympathy of a woman who was so useless she couldn't even offer comfort without acting like a clumsy puppet galumphing through the china and crystal department. If the truth were known, Cole was probably far better adjusted to the inequities of life than she was, and that galling pill was the most bitter of all to swallow.

"You're doing it again," his voice announced in the heavy darkness, the tones deep but with an undercurrent of gentleness.

"Doing what?" she asked involuntarily, hating the ease with which he could manipulate her.

"Rubbing over your eyes and then your hair. You always do that when you're upset or nervous."

"I know." She dropped her hands to her lap and gripped them self-consciously. "Hannah tells me to stop at least once a day."

"At least she's good for something. Come over here."

"What?"

"Undo that seatbelt and come over here next to me. There's one here so I'm not asking you to take any undue risks." His voice was still gentle and teasing, but there was an unmistakable order couched in there that Sheila found she couldn't ignore. The blood was roaring through her veins like a runaway steam locomotive, pounding out an erratic and dizzying message as she found the latch and then released it. His arm came around her shoulders and pulled her close as she slid across the seat, smoothing the tense muscles with the skill of a professional masseur. "Honey, nobody saw you spill that water, and even if they had, it was an accident that could happen to anybody. As for my brother . . . it happened a long time ago and any pain is long gone. He's dead and my parents are dead, but I'm not going to spend the rest of my life in mourning." He hugged her, then administered a slight shake. "Your Christianity ought to tell you that, if I remember rightly."

"It does, and you do. It's just that you've hit me with a lot of things about yourself I didn't know before."

"Ah, yes. My dramatic confession." He drove in charged silence for a few minutes, his fingers now stroking the hairs that curled riotously around her neck and ears almost absently. "You know, I find you an amazing woman, Sheila. Even last August when the accident happened, you didn't even try to find out who was responsible. Most people would have taken me to the cleaners, and I even instructed my lawyer to plead no contest if you pressed charges. And now, after I've seen you almost hysterical with fear and then all but accusing me of murder in a moment of anger, you tell me it's not my fault and that you don't hold me responsible for your blindness."

Cole pulled into Sheila's driveway and shut off the engine. In the sudden silence she could hear a cricket out in the back yard, and across the street a whip-poor-will called its mate in endless repetition. Then Cole's hands were cupping her face. "If you can forgive me for what I did to you, my frightened little doe, then why can't you forgive yourself for your fear?"

117

CHAPTER 7

THE INCESSANT DRONE OF A LAWNMOWER intruded in the quiet of a fresh spring morning, but the heady aroma of fresh-cut grass more than compensated for the noise. The sound had to be coming from the Ericsons' yard; they were the only family on the block who insisted on trying to maintain a lawn before the rugged winters in the ancient Blue Ridge Mountains of Virginia finally yielded to gentler weather. Everyone else was just now planting grass seed and spreading fertilizer, but Larry stuck with his winter rye for the pleasure of having to mow the yard in late April.

Sheila stretched her cramped limbs, feeling as warm and lazy as the Oates' tomcat. The sun was baking her head and back where she had been sitting in the lawn chair, and she was wearing sunglasses even though she was still blind. "The sun could easily finish what your accident started," her doctor had counseled her, "so even when you can't see and you're out in the sun for extended periods, wear your dark glasses anyway." With a weary sigh she pulled them off, and in an absent-minded gesture, started to rub her eyes until she remembered the previous night and Cole's last observations.

"Oh, drat it all, anyway!" she exclaimed aloud in annoyance, yanking the offending hands down and in her irritation dropping the sunglasses. She leaned over and groped around until she found them, felt a sudden swift stab of pain over her eye, and when she straightened, her vision had come back.

For a minute things were blurred and the colors all washed together in soft pastel hues and then, like a camera with a self-adjusting lens, her vision once again clicked back into blessed sharp focus. "Oh, thank God!" she breathed, bowing her head and clasping her hands in fervent appreciation. Then she gazed around, soaking up sights like a thirsty sponge and without any conscious volition, words started dancing across her brain. . . . Showers of sunlight, hazy, lazy colors that spread a song upon the heart. . . . She rose to her feet, feeling the inspiration gushing forth like a clear bubbling fountain and filling her with an excitement that had been missing for months. Light as the sunbeams, she dashed into the house and made a beeline for the typewriter.

Hannah, unloading wet clothes from the washer and shaking them before tossing them in the dryer, froze in mid-toss as Sheila disappeared into the study. "What is it?" she called out when it became obvious that Sheila had not even noticed her presence.

"I've got an idea!" Sheila yelled back over the sharp staccato sounds of the typewriter. "And by the way—I can see again!"

"I noticed." Hannah went back to work, but now her plump face was wreathed in smiles. Sheila hadn't sounded that lively and enthusiastic since Hannah had come to live with her. Maybe the light at the end of the tunnel had finally appeared. "But I sure do hope it's not that man," she muttered in a wrathful undertone, slinging a pair of innocent jeans into the dryer with undue force. "It would make that light an oncoming train, I'm afraid." She shook her head, feeling a misgiving deep inside that was as annoying as her infrequent twinges of arthritis. Her smile faded, and she finished loading clothes in thoughtful silence, the only sound the rapid rhythmic tattoo of the typewriter.

Daylight was fading to a deep lavender twilight before Sheila wandered dreamily out of the study and into the kitchen. Hannah was at the sink, chopping up potatoes and celery for potato salad, and Sheila noticed a fryer washed and cut up on the counter. "You make good fried chicken," she announced cheerfully, and Hannah glanced over her shoulder briefly.

"Well, I've been doing it long enough," she smiled at the younger woman. "I was beginning to wonder if I'd have to fry it under your nose to get you out of that study. What are you working on, anyway?"

Sheila sat down at the kitchen table, plopping her chin down in her hands. "An inspirational poem," she confessed, smiling a little at Hannah's predictable response.

"Praise be—I knew you'd be back to it sooner or later! Now don't you feel better?"

"I don't know—yes,'" she amended, but there was a tangible question mark hanging in the air. "I'm still confused abut some things."

"You mean Cole Hampton." It was a flat statement, and Sheila sighed.

"Hannah, I know you don't approve of him, okay? You're very good with your nonverbal communication, you know. And if it helps at all, I'll reassure you that I'm more than aware that his only interest in me is pity and a dose of belated conscience."

She had given Hannah an abbreviated version of her evening out, mainly that Cole had confessed he was the driver of the other car. "I still don't

120

understand why everyone felt it necessary to keep me from knowing," she had observed at one point, and Hannah had given an inelegant snort.

"Because it was obvious every time his name was mentioned that you were infatuated with him, that's why! Besides, you never really expressed the desire to know after your attacks started, and we all felt that it was best to let sleeping dogs lie—or wolves," she had added darkly, and Sheila had had to laugh. The sound had been so startling that they had both gaped at one another for endless seconds until Hannah had turned abruptly aside. "You haven't laughed like that in ages," she muttered gruffly.

Now, as Sheila watched the stiff, disapproving shoulders of her 'watchdog' housekeeper vividly expressing some more nonverbal communication, she felt the last of her creative aura fading away like wisps of insubstantial smoke. "Would it help if I told you he's going out of town for two weeks and maybe between now and then, you can think of some anti-love potion to dose me with?"

Hannah put the huge French chef's knife down and turned around, wiping her hands on the ever-present apron. "I just hate to see you hurt," she folded her arms and regarded Sheila sadly. "It's not like you to sound bitter, honey."

"I haven't sounded like me in a long time, have I, Hannah?" She stood, wandered with restless steps over to peer out the back door. "But then I'm starting to wonder who the real me *is*. I always thought I was a pretty strong Christian, but I'm not sure about that any more. I always thought I'd fall in love with a kind, decent Christian man who would court me with pretty words and lots of romance." She watched a gigantic black and yellow garden spider inch its way stealthily down toward a hapless bug caught in its net. "Won't you come into my parlor?" she quoted softly beneath her breath, and a wistful smile curved her drooping mouth as she compared herself to that pitiful bug—although she could never compare Cole to a spider, even if he could be every bit as ruthless. "Doris told me she thought I was trying to make myself into the 'perfect example of Christian womanhood'; Cole tells me I'm a coward, and you tell me I'm a fool. So far I'm batting a thousand . . ."

"What's your poem about?" Hannah interjected hurriedly.

"Doubts, fears . . . despair, tears . . . sounds like I know what I'm talking about, too." She opened the screen door. "I think I'll go for another walk, Hannah. But I promise to stay in the yard where I belong. Call me when supper's almost ready, and I'll set the table."

Time passed slowly, each day meandering through the hours like a sluggish, slow-moving river that wasn't in any hurry to reach its final destination. Night was longer in coming, and the temperature continued to rise. The weather, in fact, was perfect with its halcyon days and deep, still nights, and Sheila found herself staying outside more and more whenever she wasn't working. Elaine came over several times and they spent the afternoons cultivating a tan, though Sheila's skin was too fair to really brown well. "You old Southern belle," Elaine had drawled more than once. She bullied Sheila into going shopping and buying some new summer clothes, and on one balmy Sunday afternoon even talked her into going for a bike ride.

Joe and Doris came for supper twice. No one mentioned Cole, and Sheila grew rapidly weary of pretending not to notice all the meaningful glances that were supposed to be directed behind her back. It would have been a lot easier if they had just gone ahead and talked about it, let Sheila talk about it. Except they had done all the talking, everyone knew how everyone else felt, and Sheila concluded with an aching pang that her only real ally was time. Cole had said he would call her when he returned, but she was sure he had said that so many times before, it was probably a meaningless ritual by now.

She had written a few more poems, and though she could see that her soul was still troubled, at least she could also see that, like a thin steel thread, her faith was still holding in spite of it all. Daniel, she knew, would be pleased. He had accepted her other lines of cards, had even made a tidy profit on some of them, but he had been as disappointed as everyone else when she quit writing inspirational verse.

"I'm trying, Lord," she spoke aloud one night, lying in her bed and staring up at the ceiling. She could just make out the dark spot where the roof had leaded one year, and that reminded her of her parents. What would they be saying to her? Would they have agreed with Cole's assessment—that she needed to accept her fear and then take it from there? And what would they have thought of Cole himself?

The phone's ringing gradually penetrated her conscious mind, and she jumped out of bed, kicking the covers wildly as she made a scrambled dash for the extension in the front hall before it woke Hannah. Nobody called at this time of night but wrong numbers, obscene callers, or bearers of bad tidings. The odds were against her, but having to cope with an agitated Hannah was better than coping with an hysterical Hannah. "Hello?" She was breathless, tentative, and there was a distinct masculine chuckle from the other end.

"Did I wake you up, Doe-eyes?"

"Cole!" The breath swooped out of her in a rush. "What are you doing? Do you know what time it is?"

"I'm talking to you, and it's—" there was a pause—"eleven minutes past midnight. Are you in pumpkin form?"

His voice, with its deep undulating cadences that poured over her like thick golden honey, hadn't changed a bit. No—it *had* changed. The bite was gone, and right now there was a husky rasp that raised goosebumps on her skin. Sheila noted with helpless inevitability that her palms were damp, and that her wit was reduced to a dumb longing just to hear his voice.

"Sheila? Are you still there, or have you fallen asleep?"

"I'm still here." She made a face at the phone and mustered a semblance of composure. "I'm not in pumpkin form, and I'm certainly not asleep at the moment, thanks to you. Didn't you know that decent people are in bed at this time of night?"

"Indecent people are in bed at all hours," he murmured wickedly.

"And I'm sure you would know." Her voice was as stringent as vinegar. "What do you want, Cole?"

There was a long pause. "Right now, I'll settle for your presence on the front steps of your house in the morning—nine o'clock sharp," he said finally, with what Sheila later decided was commendable restraint, "Wear slacks."

"Am I allowed to know what the occasion is?"

"I'll tell you all about it in the morning. I'm too tired right now—I just got in from New York and I need my beauty sleep. Sweet dreams, honey." And he hung up.

Sheila went back to bed fuming, her mind running over innumerable plans for revenge, at the same time trying to come with some new words to describe such an impossible arrogant, aggravating man. But her mouth wore a smile that wouldn't go away, and the face in the bathroom mirror where she had gone to get a drink of water was fairly blooming. All the doubts, fears, and warnings went scurrying under the bed with the rest of the unwanted dust. He had called her after all, and he was coming to see her in the morning.

His eyes ran over her in narrow, piercing thoroughness while he watched her walk slowly down the steps toward him. "You look better—" his mouth widened to a grin, "—and I see that you can see at the moment."

Her own eyes were taking inventory, too, moving from the soft chambray shirt open at the neck to the worn and faded jeans that molded themselves to his sinewy athlete's legs like a second skin. Her eyes returned to the strong column of his throat and the sprinkling of crisp hair revealed above the open collar. When she finally managed to drag her gaze to his face, her eyes were caught in a silver snare that somehow managed to elate and frighten at the same time. "I imagine you're used to women staring at you," she remarked in a gruff, subdued voice.

"Honey, it's so nice to know that you *can* stare at me. The fact that other women do is totally irrelevant." He held out his hand and after a brief hesitation Sheila placed hers in it. With a smooth swiftness that caught her completely off guard he tugged her into his arms and held her close. "Of course, the plan I've concocted for you doesn't depend on whether or not you can see."

"What plan?" She dared not struggle because she knew it would only make things worse: she had just noticed Corrie Oates and Kimberly Rinero watching them in unabashed fascination from Corrie's front steps. "Cole, I want you to know that you're ruining my reputation." She managed to extricate one arm and gesture in the general direction of the house across the street. "Inside of thirty minutes the entire community is going to be under the impression that I've been swept off my feet by a tall, dark, handsome stranger . . ."

"Hmm . . . not a bad idea. Let's go." He stopped slightly, slipping one arm beneath her legs, and before she could draw another breath, she was in his arms

125

and he was striding to his car with the boldness of a swashbuckler.

Sheila closed her eyes and groaned; she could hear Corrie and Kimberly shrieking with ten-year-old glee, and from the doorway she also heard Hannah's smothered gasp of indignation. Cole deposited her with a grandiose flourish on the front seat, gray eyes now molten pools of silver laughter. Her eyes flew open as he dropped a kiss onto her nose, and the laughter that had been restrained for so long gurgled up and spilled over. "You—" she choked out between giggles—"are impossible!"

They drove off down the street at a decorous speed, and Sheila cast her fate to the winds. She might as well be the star attraction at a circus, since Birdie was just unlocking the door to the post office and looked up as they drove by. Between Birdie and Corrie, the entire county from here to Roanoke would know that Cole Hampton had just carted her off at nine o'clock on a Saturday morning.

"Where *are* you taking me?" she finally asked, idly scanning the interior of his car. At least she knew now that it was a burgundy Chrysler New Yorker and every bit as luxurious to look at as it was to feel.

"You, my lucky lady, are going to experience the treat of a lifetime. I'm taking you flying in my Cessna."

"You're *what*?" Surely she had misunderstood. Sheila had never been farther off the ground than the Ferris wheel at the state fair in Richmond, and even then she had wound up so dizzy and disoriented that she had had to be led to the nearest hotdog stand where she could sit down and sip a Coke. She knew it was unheard of in this day and age never to have flown in a plane, but there had just never been any reason for her to use that mode of transportation. All her relatives lived within a hundred-mile radius, she had gone to college in Lynchburg, and . . . well . . . she had never even wanted to fly in a plane.

"Flying, Doe-eyes. Flying. Up in the sky as free as a bird. Up with the clouds, where you can look down at earth and all you problems suddenly turn out to be just as small and insignificant. You'll love it." He spoke with the enthusiasm of a small boy showing off his favorite toy, the chiseled angles of his rugged face sharp with excitement.

Sheila pondered his profile silently for a moment, inwardly debating what her reaction should be. "I've never flown before," she revealed after awhile to the windshield wipers, her voice idle, speculative. "I don't know whether I'll like it or not."

"Never flown in a small plane, or never flown?"

"Never flown, period. And before you pass out and drive us off the road into the ditch, I'll explain that it's lack of opportunity, not the attitude that 'if-God-meant-for-us-to-fly-He'd-have-given-us-wings.'"

"No problem, either way." His voice was disgustingly cheerful and careless. "You'd still be going flying, regardless." He looked across at her and grinned. "This is one of the many firsts I plan to show you, my wide-eyed innocent. Relax and enjoy it."

Sheila refused to rise to his provocative bait. "Cole . . . why are you doing this? And don't feed me the line about how irresistible I am, please. I may be 'innocent' in your eyes, but I'm not dumb."

His countenance sobered, and they drove for almost another mile before he answered. "I'll tell you when we get to the airstrip. I don't want to talk about it while I'm driving."

After that uninformative but rather unnerving pronouncement, they drove the rest of the way in silence. It was only about five more minutes, actually, because Cole had driven out to the small airstrip used mostly by cropdusters instead of the airport in Roanoke. As if he could read her thoughts, Cole explained as he pulled in front of a small metal building and stopped, "I keep my Cessna here. I have a larger one, a jet

127

actually; that is in Roanoke. That's for business. This one is strictly for pleasure." He shifted in the seat, facing Sheila directly now and watching her in that intimidating manner that made her feel like a mouse confronting a hungry Oliver. "So. You want to know my motives." His fingers drummed the leather-wrapped steering wheel as his gaze grew even more speculative. "Y'know, most women wouldn't have to ask that question, and for every other woman but you, I wouldn't have to explain. First of all, any intentions are entirely honorable. I'm not looking to have you as a bed partner at the moment, which in itself is a radical change in motive for me. I have to confess I feel a little awkward."

"*You* feel awkward?" Sheila mumbled, wishing she could dive under the seat and merge with the teal blue carpeting. Did he have to be so blunt about it?

He smiled faintly in acknowledgment of her embarrassment, but the gray eyes didn't soften, and the smile was not a comforting one. "You bug the daylights out of me, Sheila Jamison, and I'm determined to alter that irritating state of affairs no matter how long it takes." He laced his fingers, drew his knee up in callous disregard for the upholstery and clasped it between his hands as his foot rested on the seat mere inches from Sheila's thigh. "I told you once that I kicked around a lot after my folks were killed and ended up in Vietnam." He waited until Sheila nodded her head before continuing. "Enough has been said over the last fifteen years so that I don't have to try and describe the horror of it all, but it wasn't the horror that really got to me. It was being helpless to control my circumstances, my inability to do what I saw ought to be done." He paused, and his voice went flat and expressionless. "I swore if I got out alive that I would never let that happen again. Never would I allow circumstances to kick me around like some brainless puppet without will or intelligence. I had more or less given up on life when my parents died—didn't care whether I did or not, and didn't care *what* I did, period. That's no way to get through life, but I had to learn the hard way." He sighed deeply, and his eyes closed to give Sheila a few seconds of relief. A few seconds was all she had, because when they re-opened they zeroed in on her again, with an intensity that chilled to the bone and burned like a laser beam. "I came back from that living hell with what I suppose you could call my philosophy of life: I could do anything, be anything I determined to be, and nobody had the right to tell me what to do unless I gave it to them. I saw a future developing in computers and electronics, so I went back to school, got my degree, and never looked back.

"'I am the master of my fate, I am the captain of my soul . . .'" Sheila quoted half under her breath. She remembered snippets of information gleaned over the years about him, how he had received degrees in both engineering and computer science, on top of participating in most of the collegiate sports the school offered. How he had started his company on nothing but a shoestring and sheer gumption and transformed it into its present level of success in less than a decade. . . .

"What did you say?" Cole was demanding, a suspicious glint in the gray eyes.

"I was quoting from a poem I heard years ago, when I was growing up. What you're saying reminded me of it." She hesitated, then added bluntly, "I can also see what all this is leading to. You think I've let my problem take hold and control me, that I'm a weak-minded puppet and a spineless coward who doesn't even have the courage of her convictions."

"As a matter of fact, yes, I do." He was blunt, too, but it was nothing more than she had expected. Cole never had been one to mince words or spare feelings, and he called the shots as he saw them.

Her whole body was numb, heavy as if a hundred-weight of earth was pressing her down, down until she would be buried beneath it. "So what was your grand scheme—force the poor blind fool to face her nemesis and overcome it like you did? Transform myself into superwoman and take on the world?" The words sounded like someone else was saying them, and even as they spilled forth she could hear another voice inside her saying, *You don't need to be a superwoman to take on the world, Sheila, and you don't even need to struggle alone like Cole has done. All you need is Christ. Let Him take control again, and you'll be the victorious woman I created you to be.*

"Sheila!" She realized then that her eyes had closed and that Cole had slid over and was now gripping her shoulders, shaking her firmly. "You've got to face it," he was saying forcefully. "I'll *make* you face it no matter how much it hurts."

She opened her eyes, gazed steadily into his with an expression of such deep misery that Cole winced. She ignored it. "I understand," she replied in a dead monotone. "You do carry your feelings of pity beyond the call of duty, don't you?"

Veins bulged in his temples, and there were two hard white ridges digging in on either side of his mouth. It was patently obvious that Cole Hampton had worked himself into a rage. "Think what you like," he growled in rigid control. "But I plan to force you out of your fear and your boxed-in existence and teach you how to be a woman again—beginning right now!" The gray eyes flashed once like two sharp sabers, then he released her, got out of the car and disappeared inside the metal building. In his wake he left a palpable aura of anger, and Sheila couldn't control the shiver that started at the base of her spine and rippled out to the tips of her trembling fingers.

Cole appeared a little while later with another man—a thin, lanky fellow wearing overalls and a baseball-style cap covered with greasy splotches. They disappeared around the end of the building, and Sheila saw with a sinking heart that Cole was still angry. She was already nervous—she didn't want to go flying with a man who was mad enough at her to pitch her out of the plane if she was unable to come up to his expectations. She felt like she had fallen into a bottomless pit, and with this desperation clutching at her, she bowed her head and closed her eyes, praying as she had never prayed before. There were no pretty words, no pat phrases, no attempts to present herself in a manner pleasing to her Master. *Help me, God, please help me*, she cried from the tortured depths of her soul. *I've quoted and memorized and tried to claim all those promises You gave us, but I never needed them like I do now. If I can't gain control, if I can't give in and let Christ take control, I'll be failing You as well as Cole. Oh, Lord, I do believe. Help Thou my belief.*

"Come on. Crying isn't going to make me change my mind."

He had opened the door and was standing there, glowering down at her. Sheila opened her eyes, took a deep breath, and got out. A stiff breeze whipped the hair into her face and the morning sun was blinding. "I'm not crying," she told him with quiet dignity. "Actually, I was praying."

He took her arm, and they began walking back around the other side of the metal building, although Sheila felt more like a prisoner being frogmarched to her execution. A corner of her mouth tilted.

"Did it help?" he asked, sarcasm undisguised.

She looked up at him, and an expression of wonder filled her face. "As a matter of fact, it did," she replied, and was filled with sense of tremulous surprise.

"Good. Then I won't have to endure hysterics or any display of air sickenss during our first lesson."

"Lesson?" she queried, and some of the inner serenity faltered.

"That's what I said. You're going to learn to be in complete control of your environment, Doe-eyes, and though I won't expect you to do much on the first run, I am going to let you have the controls for a few minutes so you can—"

"Do you have a death wish or something? I may never have flown, but even *I* am aware that you don't just hand over the controls to someone who doesn't know what to do."

"No, I don't have a death wish, nor am I a complete fool. I know what I'm doing, Sheila."

They had reached the plane, and to Sheila it looked pitifully fragile, like an overgrown dragonfly which a mere puff of breeze could swat out of the sky. Cole turned her, gripping her forearms as he searched her face. "Will you try to trust me a little, honey? I swear I won't let anything happen to you."

"A little while ago I thought you might be entertaining ideas of pitching me out of the plane to make— uh—my 'mark' in history." She laughed, but the uncertainty was still in her eyes.

Cole grimaced, lifted one hand to skim his fingers along the smoothness of her cheek. "I'm sorry. You do make my angry, as I believe we've ascertained before, but I believe we also ascertained that I have no planes for you that include your untimely demise." The gentle fingers balled into a fist and chucked her lightly under her chin. "Don't be frightened, honey. I'll take care of you."

"Someone else is, too," she asserted tranquilly, but inside, her heart was starting to race.

Cole shot her a cynical look, then proceeded to lecture her on some of the basic mechanics of flying a light "prop job," as he called the twin-engine, four-seater plane.

Taxiing down the runway wasn't bad, but as Cole revved the engine in preparation for take-off, Sheila felt a gargantuan lump that was resting heavily in her churning stomach and traveling upward to her throat. *Help me, Lord,* she mouthed silently again, not noticing the piercing appraisal of the man beside her.

"Here we go," he announced easily, and the wind whistled past, the propellers roared, and they went soaring into the sky with the grace of an eagle. Well . . . maybe a Canadian goose. Fear and wonder and hysteria were running neck and neck in the race for dominance. Sheila bit her lip, dug her nails into her hands and forced herself to look out the window. The same wordless prayer repeated itself in a litany until she felt a warm hand on her arm.

"Are you all right?" Cole shouted above the throbbing noise of the propellers.

Pinning a smile on her face, Sheila shouted back, "I'm fine. Where are we going?"

"We'll just be doing patterns in the local area today, and maybe a few touch-and-go's for me. I haven't had a chance to fly this baby in a month now." He shot her an infectious grin and winked. "It's a great feeling, isn't it!"

"I am certainly having some feelings!" Sheila agreed, then gasped when Cole swept into a steep left bank. Her stomach felt like it had gone the other way, and for one horrible minute she entertained the bizarre image of having to throw up in her purse, which looked to be the only available receptacle. *Oh, help me please,* she breathed, and the queasiness passed.

They had been in the air for about thirty minutes when Cole began telling her about the controls, pointing to them and making her repeat their names. He showed her how to use the rudder pedals, the radio, the dual yokes that reminded her of the steering wheel on a child's toy automobile . . . the altimeter,

133

the compass, altitude indicator . . . vertical velocity indicator . . . the names all ran together, but after awhile Sheila was astonished to realize that she was gaining a rudimentary knowledge and pretty fair idea of what it was all about. "You're a good teacher!" she shouted at Cole, who merely grinned.

"We're about to find out," he replied, sitting back and taking his hands from the yoke.

"Cole!" Her voice rose to almost a scream. "What are you doing! I can't—"

"Take over, honey. You can do it," he instructed, crossing his arms nonchalantly. "Just head for that water tower straight ahead." When she made no move, he picked up one hand and placed it on the yoke in front of her. Within seconds the plane dipped violently.

"Cole! Help me! I don't know what to do!"

"Just pull her up gently." His voice was calm.

She obeyed and, to her amazement, the nose of the plane responded instantly.

"But, Cole, I don't know how—"

"Just sixty seconds, Sheila—one minute—and I'll take the controls back." His voice was velvet-covered steel and his will was as irresistible as the tide. "Give yourself a chance. Break loose from your fear and breathe again."

Shakily she placed her other hand on the controls, forced herself to relax and follow the movement, but she was relieved to see that Cole had returned one hand to the yoke in front of his seat and was surreptitiously guiding the airplane.

"That's it . . . good girl. . . . "

After a few minutes she relaxed enough to be able to feel the control she was exerting over the aircraft, and was so delighted that she didn't even notice when Cole removed his hands completely. Only when she chanced a quick look in his direction did she realize that she was actually flying the plane all by herself.

Instant panic erupted as she gasped, jerked wildly, and then pulled her hands from the yoke as if it had been a snake.

Cole burst into uproarious laughter, settled them back on a steady course, and then held out his hand, palm up. "Give me your hand." When Sheila slowly obeyed, his own closed over it and he lifted her fingers to his lips. "Congratulations, my love. You're on your way." Their eyes met in a wordless communication that sent Sheila's heart soaring far above the meager height of three thousand feet.

Cole released her hand after a minute and turned his attention back to flying. The relaxed smile on his face was wiped off with the abruptness of the click of a camera shutter, when his eyes scanned the instrument panel. The rough curse emitted from between suddenly clenched teeth was more than enough to send Sheila's heart tumbling all the way back down to earth.

"Cole? What is it?"

A mask settled over the grim countenance, and he didn't reply for a minute. "We've got trouble," he announced finally in a perfectly level voice. "Something has caused the oil pressure to drop, and it's making the engine temperature rise." There was a fractional pause. "There's only one option in a case like this—I have to pull the throttle to idle or the engine will overheat and quit anyway."

"We'll have to crash-land, then," Sheila finished, and incredibly, unbelievably, flashed him a small smile. "I've seen all the *Airport* movies. Tell me what to do, Cole."

If they survived she would carry that look of unconditional approval and pride he bestowed upon her for the rest of her life. If not . . . well, she could carry it to her grave. She listened carefully as he issued terse instructions, following them instantly and maintaining as calm a facade as possible to allow him all the concentration he would need. The cessation of sound was eerie, frightening, but in another sense it was also awesome; at this moment Sheila was very close to God.

"Are we going to die?" she asked at last, not even the hint of a tremor betraying her as the plane glided in a rapidly descending circle toward the earth. It seemed to be approaching awfully fast.

"Not if I can help it. See that meadow?" He inclined his head slightly. "It's fairly level, and that's where we're headed." There was absolutely no expression in his voice; he might have been discussing the annual stock report with his vice-presidents.

Sheila feasted her eyes on the narrowed intentness of his eyes, the determination of his jaw, the rock-steadiness of his hands. And she knew that if anyone could land them safely in that meadow, Cole Hampton could.

"Okay, honey, we're going in. Put your head down, like I told you, and make sure you keep it covered. The minute we've stopped completely, you get out and run."

"I will, Cole." She licked her dry lips, tried to swallow. As the ground rushed up at them at what seemed to be an impossible speed, she closed her eyes, her lips moving soundlessly now in prayer.

It happened so fast she never could remember any details beyond the spin-wrenching, bone-jarring bouncing and the unnatural sensations of speed and silence. Something slammed into the side of her head, and it was only then she realized she must have lost her balance and moved her arms some way. There was a roaring in her head and a blinding brightness, but she wasn't having an attack because she could still sense the presence of colors. The awareness that they had stopped slammed into her now and she was fumbling for the seatbelt with fingers the size of sausages. Suddenly she was being lifted, carried away from the suffocating confines of the plane and finally the roaring in her head dissipated and she could hear someone calling her name. She opened her eyes and looked straight up into Cole's. They were black, and his brows were drawn together in a ferocious scowl. Sheila reached and touched them with shaking fingers, marveling at their texture, their reality.

"What do we do for my next lesson?" she whispered in a low voice as shaky as her fingers. Her smile, however, was unfeigned and she watched in relief as the ferocious scowl lightened even as the arms holding her snuggled her even closer.

"I thought we'd try something a little more exciting." Cole drawled in a deadpan voice. He reached into his pocket and drew out a snowy handkerchief, pressing it gently to Sheila's forehead.

"Am I hurt?" she asked, only now beginning to feel the throbbing ache.

"You've got a cut on your forehead, but it doesn't look too bad." He smiled at her reassuringly. "I guess I have to apologize. I promised you wouldn't get hurt."

"Well, although I can truthfully say I look forward to going to heaven, I am glad it wasn't today. A measly little cut I can handle." She drew in her breath. "Thank you for saving my life, Cole."

He watched her for a long moment, a look on his face she couldn't fathom. "It's only fair," he offered at last. "I've already tried to kill you once before."

CHAPTER 8

SHEILA FLINCHED AT HIS WORDS and Cole apologized immediately. "I suppose I'm a little rattled right now," he confessed, then grinned a rueful, lopsided grin. "This isn't my usual method of landing a plane."

"What happened?"

Cole helped Sheila to sit up and hold the handkerchief with her own hand, but his arms were still wrapped around her and she was supported against his chest, his knees spread, propped on either side of her like armrests. Warmth and a tangy odor of perspiration and aftershave filled her nostrils as his strength and protection cradled her in such a comforting womb that Sheila was disinclined to even the pretense of indignation at its intimacy. It the truth were known, she was finally starting to recover from the shock of an emergency landing and the reaction set her entire body quivering like a bowl of Jello in an earthquake.

"I don't know why, but we ran out of oil, which results in engine seizure if you don't shut down the throttle as I did, which means we landed in this happily convenient meadow instead of on the air-strip." A look of savage intent crossed his face. "But I have a feeling I know the responsible party, and you can rest assured he'll be hung out to dry by the time I finish with him." He looked over Sheila's tousled head toward the plane, and she felt him shrug. "Ah, well, I suppose it's still my fault for taking his word that he had checked everything out. See what happens when you depend on other people?"

"I depended on you to land your little play-toy safely," Sheila pointed out, and was rewarded with a playful tug at her hair.

"So you did." He lifted her face, gently removed the red-stained handkerchief and examined her head. "The wound has stopped bleeding. Does it hurt?"

"Not really. I—I feel sort of floaty, unreal, as if all this were happening on television or something."

"I think you're suffering a little from shock." He smoothed wisps of damp hair from her face with gentle fingers. "Sheila, I really am sorry your intro-duction to the joys of flying was so traumatic. This is highly unusual, you know."

"So are you, Mr. Hampton." She flashed a pert grin he had never seen before. "Life is never dull around you."

"That's precisely the point I've been trying to make. Will you admit I'm right, even if I ended up illustrating my point a little more graphically than I anticipated?"

"Certainly not. You're arrogant enough—Oh!"

"What's the matter?" His hand cupped her chin as his eyes searched the suddenly pale face.

"I—I had a pain. A sharp, stabbing pain . . . it's gone now." Her voice, her eyes were filled with fear, the body that had been so soft and relaxed was stiff. "Cole . . . I don't want to be blind."

"Shh . . . I'll take care of you. It's okay." He stood, lifting her easily. "Let's get you to a doctor, though, just to be on the safe side."

"Where are we? You can't carry me—I'm too heavy!" Her voice was agitated, breathless as she allowed the fear to suck her into its destructive whirlpool. She should pray—it had worked on the plane—but she wasn't as worried about imminent blindness then.

"You weigh about as much as a load of cotton candy, and we only have to walk about half a mile." He smiled down into her eyes, held her close against his heart. "We're on my land, honey, and my home is on the other side of that stand of trees. I won't have to carry you much farther than the day I fished you out of the lake."

"I'm not b—blind right now. I can walk."

"Hush. I've got you, Sheila, and I'm going to take care of you. Close your eyes and relax."

"Yes, of course." From somewhere within her deepest subconscious, the litany resumed, chanting the desperate plea over and over until it gradually fought free of the murky whirlpool and the words surfaced to her conscious mind. *I'm doing it again, Lord. Please help me like You did on the plane. I'm so frightened, and so ashamed of it.*

"You weren't this afraid when you thought there was a chance we both might be about to die in a plane crash." His voice was soft, non-threatening, and there wasn't even hint of strain from carrying her. He was striding along, his steps sure and smooth, his feet making little noise in the long meadow grasses. "Does your head hurt that much?"

"No," she admitted. "It was just that one moment. But I was afraid—" she stopped. Cole continued walking, waiting for her to continue. "I know you don't understand, but I really wasn't afraid to die. I'm just afraid of the blindness."

"You're right. I don't understand, but I also believe you." He shifted her a little, his hands adjusting to a firmer grip. "I watched you, you know, and it was really amazing. You were so scared when we took off you were green, but I could see you conquering the fear, see you starting to relax and enjoy the whole experience. And then, when I told you we'd have to land in the field and you asked if we might die—and there wasn't even a flicker of fear—that was something, lady. And you're right, I don't understand it." He stopped, staring down at her, the gray eyes searching hers restlessly. "How can you look death in the face with that kind of courage, and yet live the life of fear that you do?"

"As a Christian I'm not afraid of death because it's not an end—it's a beginning. I'll be united with my Savior, my parents, and everyone else who believes in Christ. Actually, I look forward to heaven and the day when I won't be seeing through the glass darkly, like the Bible verse says. I'll finally have all the answers to all the questions." She sighed faintly. "But as a human being, well, I told you—I'm having difficulty adjusting. I know what I need to do, and it's not necessarily what you think. I need, to quote a trite but very true phrase, to 'let go and let God.'" She kept her own gaze as open and candid as she knew how, praying that he would see, that perhaps at least she could plant a seed. "It doesn't look like I've got the courage of my convictions, Cole, but I *am* trying."

The silver gaze held hers steadily, and the firm line of his mouth softened. "I saw that today, little one. Stop trying so hard to be the perfect invincible Christian. There are enough media messiahs peddling that message, and it never has impressed me."

Hating herself for the display of weakness, Sheila was still helpless to prevent the hot tears from sliding wetly down two fever-bright cheeks. "But it's true," she choked, tasting the bitter ashes of defeat. "A person can live that kind of life if he lets Christ have complete control. Just because I can't right now doesn't mean it doesn't work." Her voice trailed away to a wispy whisper. "You're supposed to look to Jesus as the perfect example. Not me, not any other person . . ."

"Aw—" he bit off whatever he might have wanted to say and picked up his pace. "Just forget it right now, okay? You're hurt, and you've had a pretty bad shock to your system. *I've* had a pretty bad shock to *my* system. Frankly, I'm not up for a discussion in religion and neither, my frustrated little idealist, are you." His head lowered and he brushed his lips over the tear-wet eyes and spiked lashes. "Close your eyes, I told you. Concentrate on passing your first lesson with—ahem—*flying* colors—and if you're very good, I just might tell you what I've planned for you next."

They approached the house from the back. Sheila opened her eyes when she felt Cole climbing some sort of steps, but she only had time to register a vague impression of terraces, shrubs, and flowering annuals before a surprised feminine voice broke the silence.

"How romantic, darling! You look just like a scene out of an old Errol Flynn movie, but I can't say I approve of the casting, since you obviously have another leading lady at the moment."

A tall, exquisitely beautiful young woman had risen from a brightly cushioned lounge chair and was strolling toward them with studied elegance down some side stone steps.

Sheila could feel the tensing of Cole's muscles, but there were no other obvious signs of discomfort or dismay at what Sheila would have described as a decidedly awkward moment. He continued carrying her toward the other woman without breaking stride until they were close enough for Sheila to catch a whiff of expensive perfume.

"Hello, Gabby," he greeted her casually. "*Robin Hood* was always one of my favorite old movies, and I don't see anything wrong with the casting in either the original version—or mine." Now he very slowly and carefully lowered Sheila to her feet, keeping one arm firmly about her shoulders. "This is Sheila Jamison— Gabrielle Sutton. We just landed my Cessna in the meadow because I think the d— the flight mechanic either forgot to check the oil level or didn't screw the cap on properly."

Gabrielle's rather bored expression altered to concerned dismay. "Are you all right, darling? What happened to the plane? Oh, Cole, if anything happened to you—"

"I think we can dispense with the weeping and wailing," Cole cut her off shortly. "The plane is undamaged and so am I, but Sheila has a cut on her head that needs looking after. I radioed our predicament, but while you're here, I'll let you call the mechanic and explain further while I take care of Sheila. I can file the report for the FAA later, but if you wouldn't mind . . ."

Gabrielle was a tall woman with a voluptuous figure that she knew how to dress to full advantage. The masses of red-gold hair styled to fall in natural waves about her head and down past her shoulders was enhanced by the grass-green designer walking shorts and crisp white shirt she wore. Her face had just the right amount of skillfully applied make-up to create an exotic illusion of a red-haired Cleopatra. She made Sheila feel like a grubby street urchin even though the expression on her face right now was inches away from feline. She cast Sheila one calculating glance that reduced her to the status of an insect, then turned her slanting green eyes back to Cole.

"Darling, I'd be happy to if I knew precisely what to tell him. Why don't you let me take care of . . . Sheila . . . and you can take care of the business."

Sheila felt like a scrappy bone being fought over by two mastiffs. "I can take care of myself," she managed to insert tranquilly, even with a touch of amusement. "All I need are directions to the nearest bathroom." She disengaged herself from Cole's arm and took a few steps past Gabrielle, keeping her eyes averted to hide the sudden blossoming of laughter she knew had appeared. Really, Gabrielle had no reason to reel threatened, but it was flattering to be treated like "the other woman" for the first time in her entire life.

The wave of dizziness washed over her without warming, but she had barely swayed before Cole's arms wrapped themselves around her. "Sorry," she mumbled apologetically. "This is getting to be a habit."

Cole ignored her. "If you're disinclined to help, Gabby, then by all means continue making yourself at home. I'll be driving Sheila to the hospital after we get cleaned up a little, but maybe I'll see you tonight at the party." Crunching across a stretch of crushed gravel, he carried Sheila inside without even glancing back over his shoulder at the fuming Gabrielle. Sheila knew she was fuming because she caught a glimpse of pouting lips pressed in a firm line and eyes flashing fire before she turned and flounced away.

Neither of them spoke until they reached a long hallway on the far side of the house. Then Cole paused and stared down at her with a smile that didn't reach his eyes. "I'm going to leave you in the bathroom while I go search out Ada to help you take a bath."

"Cole, it isn't necessary. I feel better—" Two long, supple fingers shushed her.

"After that I'll drive you to the hospital so they can take a look at your head and check your vision. It's been blurring, hasn't it?"

She lowered her head, wondering fleetingly why she was almost relieved that he knew and that she didn't have to try and hide it. She opened her mouth to

144

agree, but the words that spilled out instead astonished both of them. "Please don't leave me alone . . .
" Color spread in a warm tide up her throat, over the
pale cheeks. "I—I'm sorry."

"Shh. It's okay, baby. I won't leave you alone.
We'll forego the bath, and I'll just wash your face for
you, then we'll go. Sheila, don't look like that. I don't
mind, Doe-eyes. In fact, I must confess to a degree of
satisfaction. This is the first time you've given in and
confessed you needed me."

He sat her down on the edge of the huge chocolate-
tiled garden tub, keeping one hand on her arm as he
reached with the other for a thick, cream-colored
washcloth hanging with several others in varying
shades of browns on a solid brass multi-armed rack.
"You can still see right now, can't you?" he asked
quietly as he bathed her hot face, being extra careful
with the cut and slightly swollen portion of her
forehead.

"Yes. . . . I ought to call Hannah."

"I'll call her from the hospital. Who's your doctor,
anyway?"

The next hour passed in a surrealistic haze as Sheila
simply relinquished herself to the care of the capable,
efficient and utterly irresistible Cole Hampton. It was
a pleasant feeling, a not quite unfamiliar feeling that
induced some guilty pangs that Sheila refused to
examine. There was a time when she used to feel this
sensation of lightness and freedom from the weight of
the world regardless of its stress and turmoil . . . but it
hadn't been because of the bulldozing interference in
her life by a man. It was because of—it was because
she trusted . . .

"Sheila, Doris is here. I'll send her in while I have a
chat with Dr. Kohn."

Sheila glanced up from where she was sitting in the
red-orange waiting room chair. She had been exam-

ined, prodded, x-rayed, and mumbled over in a manner so strongly reminiscent of last August that time seemed to have spiraled into a tailspin. "All right," she agreed with a small smile. Cole examined her sharply for a moment, then strode briskly out a door into the hall.

Doris appeared a minute later, her face pale and strained, but her mouth smiled and her eyes embraced Sheila in their warmth a second before her arms did. "So . . . when you decide to break out of the cocoon, you certainly get carried away, don't you?"

Sheila managed an answering smile. "Well, after my first experience at flying, I think I may decide to remain a caterpillar instead of trying to emerge into a butterfly." She told Doris about the morning, unaware that with every word she was fairly blazoning her love for Cole in neon lights. "What about Hannah?" she finally queried after she had finished. She dreaded the initial encounter with the overprotective but well-meaning housekeeper.

"Joe is calming her down and using every bit of his managerial skills to keep her at your home. He's reassuring her that you are perfectly all right and that Cole is taking good care of you." She chuckled, her eyes twinkling merrily. "I think she was ready to go after him with a rolling pin for putting you in that much danger."

"I can imagine." Sheila's voice was very dry. "After this, she'll probably chain me to the bed."

"I rather imagine Cole will simply break the chain." She watched the younger woman a moment in silence, a frown etching across her brow. "You do love him very much, in spite of everything, don't you, Sheila?"

"I tried not to. I know he doesn't love me and never will, that our lifestyles are incompatible, and that it would definitely be a case of mismatched yoking." Her hand reached in spite of itself to touch the white gauze bandage covering her cut. "But for some reason God put this love in my heart, and I'll have to wrestle with it like I do the blindness, Doris. Will you and Joe keep praying for me, please?"

"We've never stopped." She rose, helped Sheila until they were both certain she could stand unaided. "I don't understand Cole either, honey, but I do know that God has a history of using the most unlikely characters to accomplish His work." As they walked slowly out toward the main desk, she mulled aloud in a thoughtful tone. "Cole has changed you for the better, Sheila, even if you can't see it yet. Maybe he's breaking the ground so God can do the rest."

Sheila skipped Sunday school that Sunday and spent the hour before church in the sanctuary. She needed the time alone, time to marshal her scattered forces so she could once again be guided by the Good Shepherd. And what better place to do that but in God's house?

Eyes closed, head bowed, she absorbed the silence, the atmosphere of reverence and familiarity that rested upon her like a benediction. She had been coming to this church all her life, and it was as much a part of her as the air she took into her lungs. The white pews with the burgundy velvet cushions, the tall multi-paned windows with the sunlight streaming through them, the smell of worn hymnals and polished wood and fragrant spring flowers form the arrangement on the altar . . .

"Be still and know that I am God . . ." The words carved into the communion table wove their way around her turbulent heart, blessing her and giving her—if not the entire portion, then at least some measure of—the peace Christ had promised His troubled disciples so long ago. She was healing at last, and though she knew she wasn't completely "cured," she could at least be thankful that she was better than she had been two days ago. Two weeks ago. Six months. . . .

"How did you hurt your head, Sheila?" Tommy Sinclair maneuvered his way to her side after the services, tugging at her elbow to get her attention. "Were you in another accident?"

"Unfortunately, yes." Sheila grinned down at him. "Guess what I did yesterday, Tommy? I went flying in a little airplane that looks like a giant mosquito, and we had to land in a meadow. That's how I cut my head. How about that, hmm? I went up in the sky, way up high, but I sure didn't land as soft as a sigh!"

Tommy giggled, his eyes large and round as silver dollars. "Wow, Miss Jamison! I wish I'd been with you." He gazed up at her wistfully then, and tugged on the inevitable bow tie that his mother always made him wear. "I sure do wish you were teaching us. Nobody can make up silly poems like you used to."

Sheila put a hand on his thin shoulder and gave it a pat. She hadn't made up a "silly poem like she used to" for a long time now, and the unbidden, spontaneous flow of nonsense tugged at her heartstrings. She missed her kids, really missed them, and at this particular moment wondered if maybe she was ready to take her class back. She would talk to Doris about it later.

Cole called her fairly frequently during the week to see how she was doing and tease her mercilessly if she was less than cheerful over the phone. On Thursday he told her to be ready at eight o'clock Saturday morning, that this weekend he was taking her sailing.

"Have you ever been on a boat?" he had asked, the smile coming over the line with tangible force.

"No," Sheila had sighed, rolling her eyes heavenward. "Are you planning to try and drown me this time?"

"The kind of drowning to which I'd subject you has nothing to do with water," he murmured in a sensual

148

rasp that licked along her nerves and sent flags of color waving in her cheeks. "But we won't talk about that now. See you Saturday morning, Doe-eyes."

"I wish you'd quit calling me that," she complained to him that Saturday as they sped down the highway in the sleek New Yorker toward Smith Mountain Lake, where, inevitably, Cole maintained a "crackerjack little sloop as smooth and streamlined as a good-looking woman."

"Why?" His arm reached across the space separating them so that his fingers could playfully flick the baby fine hairs at her temples next to the eyes in question. "Don't tell me you're one of those liberated women who are offended by such appellations because you think they're degrading!"

"It's not that. I don't mind some of the names you call me—" she blushed all the more when he laughed—"But that one makes me uncomfortable." She shrugged, turned to watch the heavily wooded hills and valleys out the window.

"Why?" Cole pursued, softly but inexorably.

Sheila wished she had never opened her mouth, but now that she had started it, she knew she'd have to give him the reason or he would never let it ride. "Well, because a doe is a female deer (Oh, Lord, why did that song have to pop into her mind now?) and deer are such beautiful and gentle creatures and it makes me wonder if you're making fun of me or—or paying me a compliment." She was twisting her hand nervously in her lap now, her gaze watching the evidence of her discomfort with a sort of resigned amusement. Her father had told her many times that it was far better to keep your mouth shut and make people wonder rather than open it and prove to them you're a fool.

"Which would you prefer—that I was making fun of you or paying you a compliment?" He was staring straight ahead, keeping his face and voice deliberately expressionless.

"I refuse to answer that. It's one of those trick questions where I lose, no matter what."

"You're wrong—" he paused provokingly—"Doe-eyes. Either way, you *win*."

He slanted her a short and inscrutable appraisal that nevertheless caused her heart to stand at attention like the rawest of new recruits. She didn't play well at this kind of sophisticated baiting, this game where your mouth said one thing while your eyes and your thoughts were communicating another.

"Uh, I like your car. It rides so smooth and quiet."

"Thank you." Now his voice was mocking. "I could afford a Rolls upholstered in mink if I wanted it, but I admire Lee Ioccoca. Anyone who can turn a dying corporation around like he did deserves all the support he can get." With another quick look accompanied by one quirked eyebrow, he then deftly changed the subject and they kept the talk generalized and safe the rest of the way to the lake.

"I hope this turns out a little, shall I say, 'less exciting?' than your last diabolical scheme," Sheila dared to tease him as she helped unload the trunk.

While Cole hefted out a huge wicker picnic hamper, she scooped up a couple of windbreakers, then turned to gaze out over the car and toward the dock where she saw a large number of masts rocking gently back and forth. Sailing seemed to be a popular sport, but Sheila's experience with it was as minuscule as her experience with airplanes. What a dull and boring life Cole must think she had led! Shaking her head in irritation at her negative attitude, she determined once again to enjoy the day and the pleasure it had to offer. After all, this was the first day of the rest of her life, as the saying went. Or, more to the point, perhaps, was the stern admonition not to be anxious for anything.

So. The sun was shining in a lapis lazuli sky, and the air was fresh and still. Sailing looked like such a lovely and relaxing pastime that it couldn't possibly harbor any of the anxieties of flying a plane several thousand feet in he air. She turned to Cole, about to make some appropriately silly remark, when the stabbing pain knifed through her skull and everything went black.

"Sheila? What's the matter?"

She heard him place the hamper on the asphalt and take the few steps to her side. Then his hand was on her arm and the other caught her chin and lifted it.

"You've gone pale. Is your head hurting?" Fingers lightly touched the cut, now almost healed, then dropped back to her chin.

She tried desperately to stay calm, unruffled. He had seen her lose her poise so many times. "It happened again. I—I can't see." She took a light, shallow breath. "It was different though. I had that pain again."

"Is it still there, or are you just unable to see now?" There was nothing of her own internal panic in the calm, unemotional voice, and the fingers holding her chin maintained the steady, reassuring contact.

Sheila managed the faintest of grins. "I'm just unable to see."

"Good. Then we can still go sailing. You've got all your other senses in good working order, so there's no real problem."

"That's easy for *you* to say!" she all but snapped, pulling free of his hand with an irritated jerk of her head. Remorse followed immediately, but she couldn't force herself to apologize. It was happening again . . . again . . . again.

"Honey." With an exquisite blend of tenderness and strength he tugged her into a full embrace, his thumbs probing behind the tense muscles of her shoulder, rubbing over the bones as if he were smoothing a balm into her skin. "Buck up, Sheila. You can do it—and I'll be right beside you so there is absolutely nothing to worry about. Why don't you try some of that praying you did last week? Isn't God always supposed to have His eyes upon you?"

There was a biting note in the remark that had not been there in a long time. Sheila wanted to curl up inside herself, cover her whole body to keep out those stinging nettles of ridicule. She stood very still, and Cole gave a hard laugh.

"I'll go load this stuff and leave you alone a minute. Don't run away." He lifted the windbreakers from her arm, and Sheila found herself counting his steps as they faded into the distance.

She felt with her hands outstretched until locating the warm, waxed surface of the car. Then, leaning on it as if trying to absorb some of its inflexibly solidity, she bowed her head, opening her heart to the accumulated years of comforting verses to provide her with a much needed buttress against both the fear—and Cole's ridicule. Like tiny candles, the verses illuminated the blackened recesses of her soul, lighting a path toward hope even as they lightened her spirit. *Thank you, again, Lord! I don't know why it's taken all this time, and maybe Doris was right: It is Cole you're using as a spur, a goad, the catalyst that forces me to live my faith like You want me to. I can feel myself breaking open to Your leading again, feel the reality of Your comforting presence even if it's not twenty-four hours a day yet. I know You're constantly on call though, Lord, and I'm working on it.*

She was even finding her sense of humor again. Oh, that felt so good—as if she had been wearing shoes that were two sizes too small and had finally managed to free her feet.

"Are you ready?"

The curtness of his voice and the abruptness of his reappearance almost dissolved the fragile bubble of peace. But she lifted her chin a notch and smiled a dazzling smile that held more than a touch of defiance as if to broadcast her own silent message. "Lead the way, Mr. Hampton. Or should I say, 'Lay on, MacDuff?' "

There was one of those short silences that fairly sizzled with emotions. Then Cole slid his hand under her arm and led her down toward the dock. "Do you happen to recall the line that follows that particular one?"

"No . . . " She hesitated, sensing a trap beneath the lightly barbed words. "It's been awhile since I read *Macbeth*." Then, keeping her own voice light and ingenuous, "But I can quote any number of passages from the Bible if you'd care for a substitute."

Suddenly she heard him chuckle and mutter something beneath his breath that sounded, incredibly enough, like "Atta girl. Push back just as hard . . . "

Cole had been right—as usual. Not being able to see did not hinder her at all from falling as much in love with sailing as she had the captain of the craft. Or would it be the skipper of the ship? She was abysmally ignorant of nautical terms.

He led her down the deck and lifted her into his— sloop, she remembered he had called it. He sat her down on the some cushions that felt like some kind of waterproof material. She chattered amiably. "Fore and aft; Barnacle Bill; bounding main . . . I'd offer to sing, but I'm afraid you'd throw me overboard before we even left the dock." She gasped in startled astonishment as a warm mouth covered hers and two hands briefly caressed the sides of her head.

"You're a nut," Cole murmured in her ear. His breath was warm, too, fresh and minty, and Sheila's body melted into a puddle of yearning that was probably more than obvious to this experienced man.

"I also make up nutty poems," she tossed back in a throaty voice that was innocently seductive. "Like . . . like . . . Will this boat float in a moat if I carry a tote over my coat—what are you doing?" Her words deteriorated to a gasp as he bent to nibble her neck in shivery little kisses.

"I'm thinking that blind or sighted, you're an intoxicating little bundle, Doe-eyes, and it's getting harder . . ."

Blind. Blind. The word was a stoplight administering a potent enough dose of bitter reality to countermand the sweet taste of desire Cole was rousing in her. For the moment she had almost forgotten that there was only love on *her* side in the little interlude. For him, the feeling was only physical, and pity. "Cole, stop it right this minute!" Her arms pushed between them and she twisted her head from side to side.

"Don't look like that!" Cole exploded. There was a tension-laden pause and then a violent rocking movement as he left her side and apparently all but flung himself to the other end of the boat.

Sheila's arms flailed wildly, and she was unable to prevent the choking sound of distress and fear that escaped her constricted throat. He was back beside her immediately, and the arms that hauled her close, though as hard as steel cords, were achingly welcome.

"I'm sorry, honey. So sorry," he whispered hoarsely into her silky hair. "Sheila, please stop trembling like that. I'm a first-class—well, I'm sure you don't need to hear it aloud." His voice continued a rough tone of self-condemnation, apologies and reassurances as he held her against the hardened wall of his chest. Just held her until the trembling eased and she knew she wasn't going to cry after all.

His hands cupped her face. "Will you forgive me?"

Her hands came up to cover his. "If you'll forgive me. I didn't mean to—to lead you on."

"Ah, Sheila," he groaned. "You wouldn't know how to lead a man on if someone handed you a script. You're a priceless jewel, a rare gem, and that loveliness shines out of you so that I can't help but want to grab it." He turned her so that they were sitting side by side, with his arm solidly behind her shoulders as he continued to speak. "I'm not used to a woman like you, and that's why I reacted like I did, honey. It wasn't your fault, okay? And regardless of how tempting a package you are, I promise I will never do anything to hurt or shame you." He picked up her hand, placed a kiss on the soft palm. "Sheila, I know how much your faith means to you, and how hard you try to live it. I admire that. I admire the way you stand up to me even when you're afraid, even when you can't practice what you preach. I wish I—" he stopped, then gave her a hard hug. "Forget it. Let's go sailing."

. . .And so she fell in love with sailing as she had fallen in love with the captain of the craft. She could feel the wind and the sun in her face, hear the slap of the waves against the hull and the flapping of the 'jib' and 'mainsail' as they were pulled over the lake, feel the throbbing rhythm of the boat as they skimmed along free as the breeze. Yes, Cole was right. She didn't need to see at all.

CHAPTER 9

THEY SPOKE LITTLE OVER THE NEXT HOURS. and it took Sheila awhile to realize how withdrawn Cole had become. Even during lunch, when he had had to end up feeding her most of the cold chicken, shrimp salad, flaky rolls even better than Hannah's . . . and Sheila had spilled half of her fresh-squeezed lemonade all over the floor ("Deck, my ignorant baby, it's called a deck.") . . . even then he had been . . . distant. Attentive, yes; informative when asked a question, yes. But somehow withdrawn and even moody.

"Is anything the matter?" she had asked once, one hand idly caressing the wood that Cole had told her was teak.

"No." His hand reached across to cover hers briefly. "I'm just enjoying the day, Doe-eyes."

"I'm so glad," Sheila intoned sweetly. "Don't feel like you have to strain your brain to entertain me or anything."

He answered the teasing insult seriously. "That's part of the reason I'm enjoying the day. I *don't* feel that I have to make a concerted effort to find ways to keep you from becoming bored. You can be a very restful person when you're not worrying yourself to death, Sheila Jamison. I'm enjoying watching you enjoy, if you want the plain truth."

It was only a partial truth but he wasn't about to confess that. A veritable war of conflicting thoughts was assaulting his insides, a war that was shaking the foundation he had laid for his life so many years before. And it was all because of the quiet woman sitting across from him, her unseeing eyes still managing to reflect a serenity he hadn't seen before. How could she create such a tranquil atmosphere, while at the same time tying him up in knots? Because of Sheila Jamison he was doubting his whole lifestyle, doubting the whole fabric of his existence. If he was painfully honest with himself—and right now his mood did border on masochism—he would have to admit that it all started with Danny, his blinded friend in Vietnam. The kind of unquestioning, confident faith Danny had exhibited had impressed him on a deep, subconscious level that he had buried deeper because it implied a dependency on a force beyond self. He had been determined never to depend on anyone but himself, and for all these years he had been pretty successful. No, quite definitely successful, and yet . . . something was missing. Something that kept him from ever feeling entirely relaxed, at peace within himself and with the rest of the world. He had always felt somehow alienated, as if it were Cole Hampton against the rest of the world, and only by staying constantly on guard, constantly in control could he maintain some nebulous sense of security.

He turned from repositioning the boom and adjusting the jib sheet back to his perusal of Sheila. Right now he had to admit with bitter irony that he would give the bulk of his fortune to understand how she had managed to combat her fear and achieve that enviable look of utter peace when he had witnessed for himself her utter panic at other times. Was there any truth to her assertions that Christianity really worked? Was the unequivocal belief that an omnipotent God created a man he claimed as his Son and that that Man was the answer to—here his mouth twisted in a wry grimace—all prayers for peace . . . was it really that important?

"Cole, this will probably embarrass you but I'd like to thank you for bringing me today. I haven't felt this contented since before the accident." A look of quick concern shadowed the lovely dark eyes. "Don't take that personally. I didn't mean to remind you—"

"You didn't." His voice was deep, quiet. "I'm glad you feel that way." He thought of the other women he had brought sailing, remembering their sultry smiles and enticing bodies begging shamelessly for his touch. He might have given out a lot of pleasure and excitement, but he had never before offered contentment to anyone.

"Are you ever wrong about your perceptions of people?" she was continuing, that hint of laughter running like a bright ribbon through her voice. "I know I fought you tooth and nail and haven't wanted to admit that you were right, but after this, I surrender. I know now that there's a lot more to life than two good eyes." She lifted her arms in a curiously abandoned gesture toward the heavens, and a smile that took his breath away flashed in the space between them. "And I'm *sure* this will embarrass you more, probably to the point of downright insult, but I thank God for you, for what He has been able to do for me because of you."

"You're right," his voice was acid, biting. "I can do without maudlin displays of emotionalism." There was the sound of straining rope and whipping canvas and the smooth sailing was interrupted almost viciously. "It's time to go back. I have another date tonight and need a little breathing space before I get ready."

There was a strained silence between them all the way back. Sheila sat quite still, berating herself endlessly for her impulsive words even as she writhed beneath the poisonous effect of Cole's venomous tongue. It would be far better for both of them if she refused to go out with him again, and as she sensed the gradual slowing of movement and heard Cole lowering the sails, she prayed for the strength to abide by that painful decision. God would provide solace and guidance from now on, and Cole could be done with philanthropy and pity.

"Ahoy, there, sailor!" called out a lilting feminine voice that Sheila recognized immediately as Gabrielle Sutton's. She stiffened her spine and hoped her wilting sense of humor was equal to the task. She heard Cole mutter something that was very uncomplimentary to women in general and that helped more than anything.

"We have a welcoming party, it seems," he grunted shortly.

"So I hear," Sheila returned equably. "Is she a little early for your date?"

"Gabby never has let a little thing like time bother her, especially when she's trying to sink her delectable claws into some poor sucker of a man."

"You, I take it, are much too intelligent to fall for such tactics?" Her arm was gripped quite suddenly with a wealth of temper evident in the bruising strength of his fingers. Startled, she pulled away, her free hand banging against the hard teak railing. "Ouch!" she caught her lip between her teeth to stifle the cry, but his hold had already eased.

"Let me see it." There was a resigned note there now, and the hand that examined hers was gentle.

"I'm fine," Sheila promised.

"In a pig's eye," was the muttered retort.

"I know you weren't supposed to pick me up until seven, but it was such a beautiful day I couldn't help but follow you down after Ada told me where you'd gone. Hello there, *Sherry*, was it?''

Cole had left Sheila's side. "Tie us up, Gabby, and quit carrying on like a gushing teenager. It's Sheila, and you know it.''

"But darling, I only met her that once, and then only for such a brief moment. I *am* sorry, Sheila.''

Sheila could imagine the look on Gabrielle's face, and she could also imagine the blatantly revealing outfit the beautiful woman was probably wearing. It would certainly outclass her simple, white duck shorts and striped, cotton knit pullover. *And I'd bet last year's royalties that she's as seductive-looking as a siren.*

She knew her attitude was less than charitable, but anything was better than the burgeoning sense of inadequacy that was threatening to topple her hard-won equanimity like a house built on sand. Wrapping herself in a cloak of aloof silence, Sheila listened with only half an ear to their banter as Cole finished securing the sails and did whatever else he had to do with the boat. Three was assuredly a crowd, and a host of phrases paraded past her to describe her miserable situation. Fifth wheel . . . dog in the manger. . . .

"Come on, honey. Let's go." His tone was surprisingly gentle, and the regret in his face would have shocked her had she been able to see it.

"She's not an invalid, Cole. Do you have to treat her like one?''

Gabby's voice was petulant, riddled with jealousy, but Sheila was in no condition to gloat or even be amused. Panicked at the woman's possible reaction of revulsion when Cole revealed her condition, she clutched at the arms that had pulled her to her feet.

"Easy, love," came his voice next to her ear. "I'm not going to tell her, but you'll have to trust me and follow my lead. Can you do it?''

"You might as well tell her. I don't mind, and I was never any good at acting." She tried to smile, tried to tell him with her shuttered eyes that she was perfectly all right. As usual, he paid her not the slightest attention. With consummate skill, he picked her up and, in an incredible display of balancing, crossed the gently rocking deck and leaped lightly onto the dock.

"Gabby, I'm not treating her like an invalid, as well you know." His voice was amused now, and fairly reeking of masculine superiority. "Since you drove your car down, I suggest you turn your charming derriere around and climb back in and follow us back to Camden. I'll meet you at home after I drop Sheila off, but right now she and I have a few things to . . . discuss."

Gabrielle laughed then, a deliciously unrestrained laugh that Sheila knew men would find irresistible. "You really are a devil, Cole, but I suppose you know that already. Very well, I'll skulk off with my tail between my legs like a chastened puppy and wait for you at your house. He's yours for the moment, Sheila. This time I'll wait my turn., although next time I won't promise to be so agreeable."

"She sounds like a lot of fun," Sheila offered after the car was loaded and they were pulling onto the highway.

"She used to be. Lately she's a royal pain."

"They why did you ask her out?" Sheila asked before she thought.

"It certainly wasn't to hear her quote Scripture and turn the other cheek. . . . " He stopped abruptly. A sigh that sounded like it had started in his toes was expelled with aggravated force. "Look—this isn't at all what I had in mind as the conclusion to our day. I apologize for Gabrielle, but I also want you to stop trying to act the noble, understanding martyr. You have a right to be . . . hurt. You have a right to tell me to take my sailboat and myself and stuff it. You have a right, my self-effacing little Christian, to indulge in the loudest, wettest flood of tears it would take to erase that—that look off your face." When there was no reply, he whipped the car over to the side of the road and stopped, thankful that Gabby had passed them long ago with a careless wave and a cynical grin. "Sheila," he ordered very quietly, "turn your head this way."

"Please just take me home." Her voice was small.

"In a minute. First tell me what you're feeling."

"I'm hurt. I feel like telling you to stuff it. I will most probably indulge in a flood of tears—at home, in the privacy of my own bedroom. Can we go now?" The lines were spoiled by the unfortunate tendency of her voice to wobble every time she paused for emphasis.

Cole started to say something, stopped, and his jaw clenched as he ground his teeth together to keep from spitting forth a round of blistering curses. Even that form of release had begun to pall. Digging the heels of his hands hard into his eyes, he then dropped one on the steering wheel; the other went to the ignition. Without another word the Chrysler growled to life.

"I'll take you home," he snapped, and pulled back on the highway with carefully controlled irritation.

He didn't call for four days. After her sight returned the day after their sailing jaunt, Sheila filled the time working. She made arrangements for Doris to drive her to Roanoke to buy some more art supplies, mailed off three new inspirational poems to Daniel, and talked on the phone with him once at his main store in North Carolina. She went to a movie with Elaine and sat in the sun. She continued her daily walks around the yard, and her heart continued to break over Cole.

"Honestly, girl, why don't you get in there and fight for the man?" Elaine had asked in exasperation. "Look at you. You're letting your hair grow whether he cares or not, you're wasting away like a Victorian heroine, you allow him to talk you into doing things that practically kill you." She licked another dollop of the triple dip cone as they say in the ice cream parlor where they had gone after the movie. "By the way, has he tried to talk you into his bed yet?"

"No. I'm the object of his pity, not his desire. He has a luscious redhead for that." Sheila pasted a smile on her face. "It was sort of flattering to have her look at me as competition, though."

"You dope. Any man with eyes in his head would rather have someone like you than all the luscious redheads in Richmond."

"If you believe that, I have some land in Florida for a good price. Elaine, would you just let it go? I'm not going out with him anymore, and besides, he hasn't called in four days now, so it's obvious the feeling is mutual." Her despair was more evident than she had intended, but Elaine took the hint and spent the rest of the evening regaling Sheila with a lighthearted dissertation of her escapades with a reporter from Lynchburg she had met a few months before.

When Sheila got home Hannah met her at the door with a forbidding cast to her face and a set to the large shoulders that promised a lecture and a half.

"What's the matter, Hannah?" Sheila asked with a resigned sigh. All she wanted was to climb in bed and bury her head in the pillow. A distinctly ostrich-like inclination, but it was there all the same.

"You had a phone call. From *him*. He demanded that you call him back when you came in. Demanded!" The double chin quivered and her voice fairly trembled in righteous indignation. "If you want some sound advice, honey, I'd just let Mr. Hampton stew by his phone until he learns that not every girl is at his beck and call. Why, in my day no man would dream of doing that, and certainly no well-bred young woman would chase after him."

Sheila's brown eyes, dark with misery, lighted fractionally at this old-fashioned diatrabe. "Hannah, you're priceless. Don't worry, I'm not going to call. But it's not out of defiance, so you can take that gloating look off your face. I just don't have anything to say to him anymore, that's all."

"How was the movie?" Hannah knew when to change the subject.

"Okay. Too much foul language as usual. I don't understand the Hollywood mentality that the only way to make money is to have a four-letter word after every four words." She rubbed her hands over her eyes, caught herself, and grimaced. "I imagine it's because the public keeps paying for it. I'm tired—I think I'll go to bed."

The phone rang.

Hannah looked at Sheila. Sheila looked at Hannah. Then they both looked at the phone perched so innocently on the telephone table, announcing to everyone within range that someone wanted to talk. Both women knew who the someone was likely to be.

"I'll take care of it," Hannah started, but Sheila held up a hand.

"No, *I'll* take care of it." She faced the other woman with a gentleness embedded in concrete. "It's my problem, Hannah." She picked up the receiver on the eighth ring and took a steadying breath before speaking.

"I'll turn you over my knee the next time you think about ignoring the phone." His voice was a low, threatening growl.

Sheila, however, knew him better after the last weeks. "Now what would you have done if Hannah had answered the phone?"

"I thought you *were* Hannah." There was a suspended moment of sweet communion in which their thoughts were completely attuned to each other. Sheila felt the laughter bubbling through her like an effervescent soda, and a feeling of happiness and well-being spilled down like a waterfall of sunshine. When he exercised that dry wit, he could cut through her resolve like a hot knife through butter. Of course, the same thing happened when he exercised a little of his potent charm, or his teasing gentleness, or his tenderness. Ah, yes, against that especially, she was lost.

"Did you have a good time this evening with your girlfriend, honey?" the furred velvet of his voice was deceptive. There were splinters of steel underneath the innocuous question, and another emotion that Sheila couldn't identify, except that it made her strangely uneasy.

"Yes, I did. What do you want?" She tried utilizing a little steel-brandishing herself.

"I'm taking the afternoon off tomorrow so we can go to Roanoke. I have a friend there's who into the Nascar racing circuit, and he's loaning the use of his car."

"Have a good time. I'll be busy tomorrow."

"I won't be able to pick you up until after lunch. I have some meetings to attend and a new computer analyst I want to check on, but I'll be there by around two-thirty."

"Do have a good time with Hannah. She's one of the staunchest members of your fan club." She counted to twenty-seven while she waited for the reply to that one.

"We're also going to have a talk about the conversation I had with Dr. Kohl this morning, as well as the most illuminating chat I had with Dr. Sanbortini Monday."

It was as if he had hurled her into a cold mountain spring without warning. "Cole . . ." she tried to drag some air into her lungs so she could say more, but he didn't give her the chance.

"I'll see you tomorrow." There was a long pause. "Sleep well, Doe-eyes."

When the doorbell rang at fifteen minutes after three the next afternoon, it was Hannah who answered while Sheila dithered in her bedroom. She put combs in her hair to hold it back, then took them out. It had grown out to where it just brushed her neck by this time, and was being as unruly and difficult as the man who had just rung the bell. She smeared lipstick across her lips and then decided it made her look like she was standing on a street corner, so she wiped it off. She was about to change from her jeans to a dressier pair of slacks when Cole's voice roared down the hallway like an approaching freight train.

"If you haven't presented yourself in one minute, I'll come back there myself—and the devil with your housekeeper!"

A bring tugging at her lips, she obeyed the arrogant summons.

"Mr. Hampton, I'll have you know that just because you are physically stronger than two women, it does not give you the right to behave in such an outrageous manner." Hannah was at her most indignant, her two chins quivering and her hands jammed belligerently on her hips.

Cole grinned down at her lazily. "I don't know, Hannah. You look like you're capable of stopping a Sherman tank."

There was a dreadful pause. "I'll be in the kitchen, Sheila." Looking as if steam were about to whistle from her ears, the housekeeper waddled in impotent fury from the living room, leaving behind a silence that twanged.

Sheila didn't waste time with pleasantries. "Why were you talking to my doctors?" she hurled at him, fear and anger vying for dominance.

"And good day to you, too, my dear." He sauntered over to her father's chair and sat down, arms behind his head, as he gazed at Sheila with a bland mask of a face. "So we're not in the mood for polite chit-chat today? Okay—have it your way. I found out that after a certain amount of persuasion that when you hit your head in our emergency landing, it apparently caused that piece of metal to shift more than it had previously." He leveled her a look then that would have stopped a charging rhino. "Why didn't you tell me, Sheila?"

She stood there, hands hanging limply by her sides and agony darkening the brown eyes to obsidian. "I didn't want you to know. What made you suspicious?"

"You'd been having some pain, and that was unusual, I knew. Before our famous landing in my meadow, you hadn't complained about any kind of pain in your head—no blurred vision, nothing. And you never had any warning when you went blind. The day we went sailing, you did. It made me wonder, and I was going to pursue it but, well, we got sidetracked. Anyway, I pursued it myself and now I want some answers." He straightened, one heavy brow cocked as he shot the question Sheila was dreading. "Why didn't you request further tests, ask if an operation was possible now? Dr. Sanbortiti admitted that if the metal had shifted as little as a quarter of a centimeter, he would be willing to operate."

"You had no right! *They* had no right—"

"No right? Who cares about rights if there's a chance you could get rid of that blasted piece of metal and not worry about going blind anymore?" He stood then, crossing to her in two long strides. "Why have you kept it to yourself? Why?"

"I don't know—because I'm not sure. Dr. Kohn wasn't sure—I was too afraid." The admission dropped between them like stones, and she stared up at him helplessly, shame drowning out the last flickers of indignation. "I'm too afraid, Cole. Like you said, a coward who can't practice what she preaches. Now will you just go away and leave me alone to rot in my

167

fear and self-pity? I'm sure I'd have an edifying experience watching you play race car driver and proving how superior you are, but—"

"There's only one thing to do when you start talking like that."

Quick as a striking snake his arms snatched her into a close embrace. With unerring aim his head lowered and his mouth stifled the angry flow of words. She fought him at first, keeping her lips pressed together and trying to push him away with her hands, but the battle was short. One of his hands captured her arms. She was forced close to him, and the shock of it left Sheila gasping.

"Sheila! What are you *doing*!"

Hannah's voice plummeted her abruptly back down the earth. She pulled free with a horrified groan and whirled to face Hannah, who was standing frozen in the doorway.

"Don't look so shocked," Cole stated with infuriating nonchalance. "I was only kissing her—nothing more."

The splotchy color in Hannah's face deepened. "I think you better go, Mr. Hampton. Sheila doesn't need the likes of you corrupting her."

"Hannah!" Sheila started to remonstrate, but Cole lifted his hand.

Gray eyes narrowed to slits, mouth a straight line, he stared at the housekeeper a full minute without saying a word until Hannah looked as if she wanted to crawl under a table. Then, finally, his expression softened. "I've promoted Sheila on more than one occasion that I would never do anything to shame her," he pronounced quietly, his gaze flicking briefly to Sheila. "I've also tried to help her see how being overly protected is just as harmful as not being protected at all."

Now he switched his attention totally to Sheila, and her heart lurched. "But I'm through forcing myself

168

and my ideas on her if my presence is that objectionable." He paused and something came and went in the raincloud depths of his eyes. "Well, Doe-eyes? This is it. The decision is up to you. Do you want to come with me or not?"

Now, when she needed his tenderness and sense of humor the most, he wasn't going to give it. There would be no pressure, no effort to sway her at all to either give in or give up. It was all up to her. She saw, as if in another body a long vista of years stretching ahead in nondescript gray if she sent him away, because Cole never made idle promises—or threats. Well, wasn't that what she had decided would be the best? The most practical? The safest, the—the most impossible?

She drew a steadying breath and met the gray gimlet gaze squarely. "'Lay on, MacDuff,'" she quoted, and her voice faltered only slightly, "'and damned be he who first cried hold, enough.'"

Ignoring Hannah's wail and aborted little flurry of movement toward them, Cole reached and lifted Sheila's cold, trembling hands and dropped a kiss on each palm. Then, never breaking eye contact, he wrapped one arm about her slender waist and led her out of the house into the radiant blue of a hot Virginia May day.

Looking back, Sheila decided that that had been the day when the rest of her "sackcloth and ashes" shell had finally gone up in smoke. Maybe it had been that passionate embrace, or maybe the shock of finding out Cole knew about the shifted metal . . . or maybe it had been her brief foray into what she knew Hannah would view as "shameful" Shakespearean quotations. But for whatever reason, *that* was the day a good portion of the old Sheila was resurrected.

On the way to Roanoke, they had sung all the wacky songs Sheila could remember, choking in laughter because Cole's voice wasn't really any better than hers. She had coined ridiculous rhymes, and Cole had topped them with even more ridiculous puns.

At the racetrack he had introduced her to "Southpaw" Sikes, who had grinned in good-natured indulgence at their hilarity as he finished polishing a fender with a chamois cloth. And when Cole had shoved Sheila into the rebuilt Impala with logos from oil companies, and auto parts manufacturers plastered all over it and informed her that it would be her turn in a little while, Sheila had mimed a hot-shot entrant in the Indy 500 and rolled her eyes. Flying around the concrete track with the speedometer hovering at one-hundred-thirty, she had grave doubts as to her sanity, but it didn't matter today. That day she was with the man she loved, God was truly in His heaven, and if all was not exactly right with the world, then Sheila refused to belabor the point. There had been no mention of her blind spells, doctors and operations, or her cowardly attitude. It was as if, for that suspended moment in time, they were just two people in love who could refuse the other nothing. The one exception to that was her adamant, mock-hysterical refusal to allow the throbbing vehicle to exceed a decorous eighty-five when she was behind the wheel.

"Southpaw has his eye on the Charlotte 500 in this charming little number, and I think he'd put out a contract on both of us if I lost control," she insisted with wide-eyed mischief, grinning at Cole from around the oversized helmet strapped to her head.

"Would that you could lose control just once," Cole intoned with a leer and a wink, but then you wouldn't be the woman I know, would you?"

It was one in the morning when the New Yorker pulled to a purring halt in Sheila's driveway, and she was fast asleep with her head on Cole's shoulder.

Consciousness returned in slow, undulating waves As she felt a warm hand gently stroking her face and hair. She opened drowsy, dream-filled eyes and stared straight up into Cole's face. There was an expression there she had never seen before, but she was too sleepy, too content to analyze it. Her lips curved in a sweet smile and her eyelids drifted down as she snuggled back against him.

What am I going to do with you, Cole thought, bafflement, frustration, and amusement playing a wrenching game of tug-of-war within his heart. She was so lovely, so pure, and he found himself wanting to believe, too, halfway hoping that he could find the kind of faith that had made her the woman he could. . .could. . .love. Did he love her? He knew he desired her, and yet there was so much more. His hand teased her soft unruly curls, caressed her ear.

So much more. He also wanted to protect her, to shield her from all the evil in the world. He wanted to take care of her. He wanted to cherish her. He wanted to be with her, grow with her and yes, he even wanted to probe her thoughts and feelings about what it meant to be a Christian.

Against his shoulder she sighed and murmured. Cole's face relaxed into tenderness, and he lowered his head to kiss her awake again.

He kissed her, a soothing, gentle kiss. "It's late. I'll pick you up at ten-thirty, so you need to get to bed."

"What have you got up your sleeve for tomorrow, Mr. Hampton? Other than bankrupting your company due to shameless neglect, of course?"

"You have an appointment with Doctors Kohn and Sanbortini, and I plan to drive you there."

She pulled away from him with a jerk, wide awake now.

"Cole, I presume that *you* presumed to make the appointment, which not only do I *not* appreciate but which I find disgracefully unethical behavior on the part of the doctors. Medical cases are supposed to be confidential."

"Since when is anything in this world like it's supposed to be?" Cole observed with weary cynicism. "Sheila, don't give me a hard time about it tonight. I promise you that the two physicians in question have done nothing to violate their professional ethics that is totally beyond forgiveness. They thought I was related to you, you see." He watched her, and in the cool white moonlight and inky shadows, she could just make out the half grin that lifted one corner of his mouth.

"Related?" she repeated carefully.

"In a manner of speaking. Dream on it, Doe-eyes, and see what kind of conclusions you can draw." He extricated himself from Sheila and the steering wheel, then reached back inside and hauled her out.

They walked to the door in ominous silence.

"Cole . . ."

"See you in the morning, honey." He kissed one last time, a sweet, lingering kiss that made mush of her bones and cold grits of her mind. Well, she would just have to borrow from the book of Matthew again and let the evils of tomorrow sort themselves out. She was really too tired and too bemused to be anxious about anything right now.

CHAPTER 10

"I TELL YOU I CAN'T! It's bad enough never knowing, but I'm just not ready to take that kind of chance right now. I *told* you it could go either way. I might end up permanently blind."

Cole braked slightly, flipping the blinker with enough force to snap it. The tires squealed in protest as they took the corner too fast, then his foot stamped on the accelerator and they shot forward. "There's a better chance you'd end up with your vision restored—just as permanently. I cannot believe that you're refusing to take that chance." His voice was flat and cold and contemptuous.

He was driving with detached concentration and barely sheathed temper. In spite of her effort not to do so, Sheila's hands clenched in her lap, and moisture beaded her brow. Cole was an excellent driver, but that hadn't prevented an accident from happening before.

"Where are we going?" she asked. She so wanted to keep him from noticing her fear. Better his contempt than his pity, because after the extremely emotional consultation with Dr. Kohn, her composure was threadbare at best. Having Cole pretending a solicitousness he didn't really feel would unravel it the rest of the way.

"We're going to a place that should make you feel quite at home." He shot her a dark glowering look. "It'll take about an hour to get there, so unless you want to crack all the bones in your hands, I suggest you try and relax. I'm not stupid enough to vent my frustrations with the car."

"You could have fooled me!" Sheila retorted beneath her breath, earning an even darker look from the man next to her. She didn't care whether he had heard her or not, keeping her gaze turned steadfastly away as she struggled to keep from hurling a barrage of words across the short space separating them. She wasn't in the middle seatbelt today.

Yes, Lord, I know a soft answer turns away wrath and I know that words spoken in anger will only come back to haunt me . . . but You know what a hard-headed, stubborn, interfering man he is! Why can't I yell at him for a couple of minutes or so? She sighed, knowing that she loved Cole too much to embroil them in a war of words where neither of them could win. Was this how married couples felt when feelings had been bruised and the channels of communication were momentarily snarled? And what was she doing, comparing Cole and herself to a married couple anyway? People had been committed to straitjackets for less insane ideas.

"Have you talked with Joe and Doris in the last few days?" Cole asked out of the blue.

Sheila glanced swiftly over at his profile, but could read nothing as the gray eyes maintained their steady concentration on the road.

"Doris and I ran some errands together a few days ago. Why?"

"Just making conversation." His arm reached and

174

he punched a button so that a radio station playing soft rock filled the silence. This time he didn't ask for Sheila's preference, and after a few minutes Sheila decided he wasn't going to say anything else at all.

After an hour's drive east toward Petersburg and Richmond, they slowed, then turned down a long driveway of hardpacked dirt. With pastureland on either side, there were neither cattle nor horses to graze its green expanse, and the wooden fence was dilapidated and desperately in need of paint. Sheila kept flicking Cole uncertain glances, that he kept ignoring. He was about as approachable as a granite boulder.

At the end of the driveway was a long low brick building with a painted sign over two freshly painted doors. The sign read "Blair Home for the Blind," and at last Sheila knew the reason for this uncomfortable journey. Her heart beating in slow heavy thuds, she turned to look at Cole with wounded eyes.

"Another graphic lesson in living, Cole?"

"Yes," he ground out with inflexible hardness. "I want you to meet some people who don't have the hope that you have—see what your fear and stubbornness might lead to."

Gathering her courage and her dignity about her like armor and shield, Sheila gracefully got out of the car without waiting for Cole to come around and open the door. He was trying to make a point. All right, she would make hers, too, and then they could go their separate ways, each convinced that the other was wrong. It would have been funny if it hadn't hurt so badly.

"Then let's get it over with," she stated with icy calm.

They didn't stay very long. Cole knew the husband and wife team who ran the home, and it didn't take but three minutes to see that they thought he was a cross between Superman and an angel from heaven.

"He's been supporting us all these years and never a month goes by that we've had to worry and wonder where the next dollar was coming from," Rebecca told Sheila with a liquid glow of gratitude plain in her light blue eyes. "We were going to have to close, you know, and place the "family" in institutions . . . and then Cole came along. It was because of his friend Danny—I'm sure he's told you—he set up a trust fund and—"

"Sheila isn't interested in all that," Cole interrupted, the faintest band of red spreading across the bridge of his nose. "She just wants to meet some of the family, like I told you. Try and understand what it's like to live in darkness every day, with no hope of any light."

"Well, now." Jasper, Rebecca's husband, was not a garrulous man and had spoken only two words since they arrived. This made four. He looked as uncomfortable with Cole's statement as Sheila felt.

"It's all right," Rebecca patted his arm reassuringly. "Cole called and explained, and I've explained to the others. It was the day you went to Richmond for—" She lifted her hands in a sheepish gesture at the look Jasper bent upon her. "I guess you don't really care about any of that. Me and my mouth . . . " She turned to Sheila. "Come with me, dear. I'll introduce you around."

I don't want to! Sheila was screaming inside. *Please don't make me! It will just prove what a coward I am. Please don't*—

"This is Everett. He's been with us eighteen years now, since way before Cole found out about us." A tall beanpole of a man stared straight ahead as his hand came up. There was a pleasant smile on his face and absolutely no hint of self-consciousness, but all Sheila could see was that he *couldn't*—and hadn't for years. She shook his hand, made some appropriate polite comment which she never could remember, and then, with a hastily mumbled apology asked Rebecca if she would excuse her for a few minutes.

Jasper was in the entrance hall, a lovely woman of about thirty beside him. "This is Rochelle," he started to introduce her, and then stopped as he caught sight of Sheila's face.

"Hello," Rochelle was continuing in a lovely melodious voice. "I'm so pleased to meet you, Sheila. Not very many people take the time to visit us. It's so very nice of you—"

Sheila could feel her heart crowding up into her throat, tears burning behind her lids as she saw in one suspended moment that lasted through eternity what she could be like in five years, what she most probably *would* be if she didn't have that operation. She would be poised, lovely, maybe even as serene and content with her lot as Rochelle seemed to be. . . . But she would never see another sunset like the one at the cabin. Never see Cole's face alight with pride and approval like that day on the plane. Never see the childish adoration in Tommy Sinclair's face.

"It's not nice of me at all," she choked out in a strangled, barely audible voice before she ran out the doors with no thought beyond fleeing to some solitary spot to nurse her bleeding soul.

She followed the sagging fence down the edge of the pasture until she reached the woods. A little ways beyond she found a gargantuan oak that had stood for hundreds of years. It was bathed in streams of sunlight that threw into bold relief the rough, gnarled trunk, contrasting with the freshness of shiny new green leaves that belied an untold number of winters successfully endured. Sheila sank between two of its upraised roots, feeling the coolness and dampness of fragrant earth on her knees as she lifted her face to heaven.

"God, oh, God!" she sobbed, tears raining down her cheeks and spilling onto the sturdy trunk. "What

177

do You want me to do? Is this Your will that I go blind forever? Or is it Your will that I see? If You want me to have that operation, You've got to take away the fear because I can't—I can't do it with all this fear inside. It's tearing me apart, Lord. And . . . and Cole. That's tearing me apart, too. Where is the peace You promised? Where is it? You promised, Lord! You promised. . . ."

For a few minutes all she could hear was the sound of her sobs blurring into the whispering silence. Then, like fragrant petals floating down and falling gently on her head, the words came. "God hat not promised skies always blue . . . Flower-strewn pathways all our lives through . . ." It was a poem from years before, from an Easter card sent to her by an old family friend who had known Sheila since she was a baby. At the time Sheila had thought it a beautiful poem, but now . . . now . . . "God hath not promised sun without rain, Joy without sorrow, peace without pain . . .

> God hath not promised we shall not know
> Toil and temptation, trouble and woe.
> He hath not told us we shall not bear
> Many a burden, many a care.
>
> But God hath promised strength for the day,
> Rest for the laborer, light for the way,
> Grace for the trials, help from above,
> Unfailing sympathy, undying love.

She had memorized and recited it in front of the church body when she was sixteen; never would she have been able to guess the impact of that poem now. For it was as if all the songs, all the poems, all the Bible verses she had accumulated throughout her life now came pouring down like the promise of God's good measure to fill her up to overflowing. There was light and lightness everywhere, in and around her and with a sensation so real she could scarcely credit it, she felt a hand touching her face, her eyes. She could hear Jesus saying to her as He had said to those blind men long ago, "Do you believe . . . be it done to you according to your faith. . . . "

Her faith. Her trust. Her obedience. All she had to do was to give herself into God's hands, and because He had promised that everything was working for her good, then regardless of the outcome of the surgery, she could be—would be—healed completely, both physically and spiritually.

"Sheila?" He had come up with silent tread and was standing a little distance away, watching her through narrowed eyes. For a minute she stayed as she was, kneeling with her back to him, but just as he started to move toward her, she rose and turned around. His breath caught and the blood seemed to congeal in his veins at the glow, the radiance of her face. At that moment she was almost unearthly beautiful, with an aura about her that seemed to reflect the brightness of a thousand suns. "Sheila?" There was wonder in the word this time and, incredibly, more than a touch of awe.

Sheila smiled at him, her smile slow and sweet and full of peace. "Take me back to the hospital, Cole, and I'll have Dr. Kohn contact Dr. Sanbortini so they can schedule me for the surgery as soon as possible." She laughed, a light, lilting laugh as delicate as wind chimes. "I've wasted two weeks already, you know."

Totally captivated by this phenomenal change, Cole continued to stare, his eyes roving over her in a restless tour as if he were trying to comprehend that this was the same woman he had brought to the Home. "What happened to change your mind?" he finally questioned, moving with deliberation until he was at her side. Where was the fear, the panic and near hysteria he had witnessed when she had run out the door? She had looked as if she were being pursued by demons, but now she looked—she looked—

"God happened, Cole." She touched his arm, then

179

with stunning unself-consciousness, picked up his hand and held it against her cheek. "God happened, and I finally learned the lesson He's been trying to teach me for almost a year." The brown eyes glowed with an inner fire that burned a hole straight into his heart as she gazed up into his face. "And it's all because of you, Cole. You can fight it and ignore it and make fun of it all you want, but you were His instrument, and I'll always—" the glow flickered, the pupils widening until her eyes were almost black— "I'll always be grateful."

Cole's expression froze, and he pulled free of her gentle hold. "I don't want your gratitude," he spoke the words with an arctic finality as the gray eyes assumed the bleakness of a glacier. "Anymore than you have wanted my pity."

They both stood under the tree, the sun still shining down upon them with warm benevolence, and though they were inches apart, they were also light years away from each other. At that revelatory moment Sheila knew that she would be able to relinquish her love for Cole to God as well, and that He would take care of both. It didn't matter anymore that it wasn't returned, because at least she had been blessed with the experience of knowing Cole, of loving him. Nothing could alter that fact nor the change in her character that had resulted. With the grace and inner serenity she had never thought to achieve, she turned at last and started walking back toward the car. "I think it's time to go, Cole, don't you?"

The night before the surgery was scheduled, Cole and the Allendres gathered around Sheila's hospital bed. The nurse had given her a sleeping pill a few minutes before and smilingly warned the trio that they would have to leave in fifteen minutes. Her smile had lingered on Cole, and Sheila teased him about it.

"I'm wondering if the nurse managed to give me the

right pill, seeing how preoccupied she was," Sheila joked, and Cole glared at her. He was still as moody and uncommunicative as he had been since the day he had driven them to Blair Home, and Sheila couldn't help wondering what he was even doing here.

"That's right, honey, keep him in his place," Joe patted her hand fondly. "Women have been falling over him far too long, and it doesn't matter if they're nine or ninety." He looked across at Doris. "It's a good thing I married a crazy woman who doesn't seem to notice."

"Oh, you mean love is blind?" Sheila quipped, and everyone but Cole chuckled. He stood on the other side of the bed, a half scowl lining his forehead and the firm lips in a straight, taut line. "You know, I've been thinking of all sorts of phrases I can use now . . . blind alley, blind as a bat . . . and of course, that famous quote, 'none so blind as those who will not see . . .'"

"There is a lot of that going around," Doris observed with studied innocence as she glanced across at Cole. Joe frowned a warning in her direction and Sheila vaguely wondered what was going on. The pill was beginning to take effect and she was feeling deliciously woozy.

"I talked to Daniel this afternoon. He's pretty excited about my latest batch." She giggled sleepily. "I hatched a batch but there's a catch; they made me itch so I had to scratch." Her eyes, so large and luminous and full once again of that joyful anticipation—along with the depth of hard-won maturity—focused on Cole now with a simplicity that caused him to shift uncomfortably. "Don't look so worried, Cole. I'll be fine, and I haven't lost my mind." She yawned, blinked owlishly. "I've found it again, actually. God is so wonderful, Cole. I wish . . . you would—could . . . " she signed deeply, her eyes drifting closed. "I just love you so much. . . ."

Three pairs of eyes met over her head.

"Now, my friend, what do you plan to do about it?" Joe finally asked, and they all looked down at the now peacefully sleeping form.

Cole felt a jumble of emotions so strong, so alien that it was difficult to speak. A look of intense agony twisted his face at the thought that, if anything happened during the surgery, he might never see Sheila again. *She* might never see *him* again. He might never hear her crack those ridiculous rhymes, never look at him with those incredible eyes filled with— yes, love. He had known for some time that she felt more for him than a fleeting physical passion or selfish desire for his wealth, just as he knew that his feelings for her were far deeper than the shallow relationships he had had with other women. He also knew that neither she nor the Allendres felt the teeth-knocking fear he was experiencing now, and his pride was shaken.

"Cole, it's plain that you love her as much as she loves you," Doris insisted very gently. "Everything you've done the last few months proclaims it. Why is it so hard to admit it out loud?"

"Aren't you worried?" he blurted out suddenly in a harsh, grating voice that betrayed the depth of emotion he was feeling. "She could be permanently blind, even die tomorrow."

"We're concerned, yes, but not worried." Joe moved around until he was beside Cole. "Listen, Cole, I'm not trying to preach or give any of us pats on the back. I just want you to—" he smiled briefly— "see. It's not a sign of weakness to depend on God. It's a sign of strength, a testament of faith. Let me ask you: Which Sheila would you prefer, the one you met at the lake, or the one you brought home from Blair Home for the Blind? One of those gave herself over into God's hands, trusting Him to take care of her regardless of what came." He laid a strong, comforting hand on Cole's shoulders, his eyes filled with understanding and compassion. "You can do that, too, Cole, if you really want to."

"Give yourself to God," he mimicked to himself the next morning as he watched Sheila being wheeled down the hall to the operating room.

Joe and Doris and Hannah were sitting quietly in three of the chairs in the sterile waiting room, but Cole was prowling as restlessly as a lion with a sore paw. How could they sit there like that? Even Hannah, the worry-wart windbag? What would happen if he "gave himself to God"? Would it really make a difference? Would he have some of that peace that was reflected in Sheila's face the day she had come out of the doctor's office and told him surgery was scheduled in three days?

Suddenly he couldn't stand being cooped up in the tiny impersonal room with its gray walls and orange and green plastic chairs. "I'm going for a walk," he growled, stabbing the elevator button with an impatient finger.

Joe and Doris looked at each other and smiled. Hannah stared after in patent disbelief.

He walked for block after block without seeing a thing. It was a cloudy day, the air wet and heavy with the promise of rain. It was the kind of day Hollywood always used when they depicted funerals—God, why was he thinking like that? God. God?

In front of him were a set of long stone steps that led up to a church. He looked at the carved wooden doors, the graceful arched windows, the soft gray stones that matched the gray sky . . . and wondered if churches were open during the week. Suddenly he wondered what it looked like inside this particular church.

The door swung silently open, welcoming, beckoning. He stepped into the narthex, stared beyond to the sanctuary. It was so quiet, so . . . peaceful. With a will of their own, his feet carried him down the wine red carpeting to the two steps leading to the platform where the podium sat. In front of the podium was a table with an open Bible, his eyes were drawn to the John 3:16 text he had heard infrequently all his life. He saw once again the look on Sheila's face when she had turned to him from praying beneath that huge oak, and then he sank to his knees and buried his face in his hands.

"Hello, Doe-eyes."

"Cole?" She was still groggy, and the pain medication they had given her kept her less than alert. But she would know that voice anywhere, anytime, and she opened the one uncovered eye and watched as his head lowered and he placed the most gentle of kisses on her soft mouth. "You . . . look different . . . " She moved restlessly, and his hand picked hers up and held it in a tight, comforting grip. "Do I sound funny?"

"You sound dopey and slurred—and absolutely wonderful." His other hand cupped her chin, the fingers caressing it tenderly. "And I love you, Sheila Jamison." He smiled at the expression in her one eye. "I have something else to share with you, but it can wait until later. Go to sleep now, honey. I'll be here when you wake up."

When she opened her eye again, the first thing she focused on was the arrangement of Easter lilies in a crystal vase at the foot of her bed. She turned her head and Cole was there, sitting in a chair beside her and watching her with—love?—in the powdersoft silver of his eyes.

"Cole?" she murmured again, and at the anxiety in her voice, he leaned up. "Did you really tell me that you loved me . . . or was it a dream and I'm making as big a fool of myself as I did the night we first met?"

He sat down carefully beside her. "It was no dream. I love you so much it makes my heart ache with it." Very slowly, very gently, he leaned over, hands on her shoulders as his mouth covered hers. It was a kiss of aching tenderness, a kiss that mingles love, passion, relief and release. "And when I realized how much I loved you and how afraid I was at the thought of losing you, I did the only thing I could do." She felt his mouth smiling against hers, felt the warmth of his breath as he drew back slightly.

"What did you do?" The words were breathless, quivering like moth wings just like the rest of her. She could hardly credit that he was hers, solid and so very masculine and saying words she had given up ever dreaming he would say.

"I gave you, and my love for you, back to God to do with as He willed." As the tears formed a sparkling pool in the deep brown eye and then spilled over, he wiped them away with fingers that trembled, then moved to just skim the white bandage covering the eye Dr. Sanbortini had so carefully penetrated to reach the offending piece of metal. His voice dropped to a suspicious huskiness. "I am so thankful, so grateful, that He seems to have chosen to give you back in my care." He cleared his throat, blinked rapidly. "So thankful that you'll be able to see the love I have for you as well as hear it, feel it. Sheila . . . Sheila. . . . " As her arms came up to enfold him, his head dropped to her chest; for many minutes they stayed thus, soaking up the other's love, basking in the peace.

"This probably isn't doing you much good," he whispered after a while in a low voice, laughter and sheepishness woven between the syllables. "Dr. Kohn warned me not to let you get excited."

"This is doing me more good than all the sleep and all the painkillers in the world. Oh, Cole, I love you so much—and I had given that love back to God, too,

because I had no idea. You never . . . I mean . . . ''
she gave up with a groan that was muffled as Cole
planted a brief but very thorough kiss on her parted
lips.

"I knew you were something different, something
special, from the moment I heard you laugh. And
when I saw your eyes, I was lost, even if it took
awhile to realize it. There was such joy, such a
spontaneity and I wanted it. I wanted you." He sat
up, smoothing loving hands over her body and
grinning devilishly at her blush. "When I saw the
change in you because of the accident—that *I* had
caused—I was so eaten up with guilt, I could hardly
function."

Sheila toyed with a button on his shirt. "You could
have been cast as one of the three billy goats gruff,"
she agreed, and he chucked her playfully on the jaw.

"I admit it," he grinned down at her cheerfully.
"Looking back I can see how God was working on me
even way back then. I was restless, dissatisfied, but
didn't know why. I guess in a way God used you as an
instrument the same way you claim He used me. I
never would have found Christ if I hadn't run into
you." His eyes dances and the entrancing grin
widened. "*Literally* run into you."

"Cole, where? When?" Her voice choked and she
gestured helplessly. "I still can't quite take it all in."

"I've been talking with the Allendres and your
pastor. They filled in all the gaps that I had only begun
to grasp when I made my peace with God. I was in
this little church while you were in surgery, and it all
seemed to fall into place."

The look in his face was extraordinary; all the
power was still there, but the relentless aggression
had been replaced by an inner peace, an acceptance
that was wonderful to see.

"I think the first seed was planted years ago in
Vietnam with Daniel Blair, my friend who was

blinded. The faith he had made an impression, but I wasn't ready to accept it then." He took a deep, cleansing breath, flexed the broad shoulders. "I am now. You were right, Doe-eyes. Christianity *does* work if you're willing to let Christ do all of it."

"Mr. Hampton, you've made me very happy." She reached up and traced the straight line of his nose, the uncompromising jaw. "I'm so happy, in fact, that my mind is spinning a billion miles an hour with verses from the Bible and poems and crazy songs about love and —"

"Well, Mr. Hampton, I see you're taking advantage of all the privileges accorded a fiance*951." Dr. Sanbortini strolled casually into the room, his white coat swinging loose and a stethescope draped haphazardly about his neck. He walked over to the bed and grinned. "Your color is surprisingly good, Sheila. Would it have something to do with your visitor?"

"Fiance*951?" Sheila hadn't heard another word beyond that one. Her bewildered gaze moved from Dr. Sanbortini to Cole, whose grin was threatening to split his face.

"How do you think I got the good doctors to divulge the pertinent medical information about you? They never would have said a word unless I gave pretty binding evidence of our relationship." He picked up her left hand and idly stroked its ring finger. "I told you, remember? You just didn't hear."

"I smell a small rat," the twinkling doctor chided as he motioned Cole aside so he could examine Sheila briefly. "Looks like my patient is still in the dark about some things, though not—" he concluded with satisfaction—"with her vision." He finished checking the bandage and straightened. "That can come off tomorrow as long as you continue to react so favorably." He turned to Cole. "You're a devious fellow, Hampton. Next time I'll know better." He patted Sheila's tousled hair and sauntered toward the door. "A nurse will be in later to check your vital signs and give you something for pain if you need it. I'll see you tomorrow."

"Sheila Jamison, will you marry me?" Cole asked promptly after the door had silently swung shut. He held her hands between his and held her one eye captive with the loving force of his gaze.

"I don't know," Sheila shot back, laughter ruining the effect. "That's a pretty backhanded proposal."

"Then we'll just have to live in sin and give Hannah apoplexy." His head dipped and his mouth began dropping tiny kisses over her face and throat. "Say yes, Doe-eyes, before I decide to do something drastic. . . ."

Her heart was singing, soaring, winging somewhere up in the midst of clouds and rainbows. "What about Gabrielle?" she teased him between kisses. "She warned me away, if you recall."

"Gabrielle was a flimsy sort of defense against your infinitely more potent powers. She knew it and I guess I knew it, but dating her was better than going off the deep end over you. Or so I thought." He resumed the kisses, lingering on the sensitive spot behind her ear, and then trailing a moist path down to the hollow of her throat. "Say yes."

"What about Hannah?" Her voice was more of a gasp now, but she couldn't resist. "Do you think your offer will cause her to retire the rolling pin forever?"

"Sheila," he growled, and his hands began tracing a burning path along her collarbone.

"Yes!" squeaked Sheila, and then for a long time there were no more words at all.

Finally Cole straightened, dropped one last kiss on her still parted lips. "You need to rest, honey, and I need some fresh air. Much more of this kind of stuff and I won't be responsible."

"I don't think I could either," Sheila admitted, and blushed.

"What happens to all that admirable self-control? No—get the light of battle out of your lovely eye. The thought of watching my beautiful, pure, bride walking down the aisle toward me more than compensates for the wait. I love you." He touched her cheek lightly, fleetingly, then rose swiftly and strode toward the door. "Sleep well, honey. I'll see you tomorrow."

Both doctors were present when the bandage came off the next day and Sheila was able to see with both eyes. She wept unashamedly, unable to come with appropriate words to adequately express her feelings. Dr. Sanbortini, a short, squat man in his sixties with normally brusque demeanor, was a wreathed in smiles as he had been ever since he knew the operation would be successful. There was something about this young woman. . . . "Make sure you take it easy for another week," he now ordered her sternly. "You can use your eyes, but limit TV watching and reading until I see you in ten days."

"I doubt if she'll be doing much of either." Dr Kohn winked at her and Sheila's responding smile could have illuminated the entire city of Roanoke.

She was sitting up, just waiting, when Cole came through the door with his usual sleek energy. He crossed the room in three long strides and scooped her up into his arms. "I see you can see," he quipped, dropping a kiss on her turned mouth. Then he laid her carefully back on the bed, grinning as she blushed rosily and frantically tried to scramble back under the covers. "*I* can see I'll have to work on your overdeveloped shyness."

"Cole," she protested, pressing her hands to the tell-tale cheeks. "You're dreadful, and I adore you."

His expression sobered as he reached into the pocket of the light blazer he was wearing and pulled out a small velvet box. With a quick flick the lid snapped open to reveal a single diamond surrounded

189

by a circle of lustrous pearls. Holding her gaze, he slipped it on her finger tenderly, then clasped her hand. "They say that diamonds are forever, but I've learned that the only thing that lasts forever is the love of God. They say that a perfect pearl is priceless, but I know that the only perfection on earth existed in Jesus Christ." He lifted her hand to kiss the ring, then each trembling finger. "But I want our love to last as close to forever as is humanly possible on this earth, and I want it to be as perfect as the three of us can make it." He smiled into her glistening eyes. "You, me—and the Lord. I've been reading the Bible and talking with the Allendres almost the whole time since I left you. My secretary is positive I've gone insane, but we Christians know better, don't we?" He paused, searched her face with that look of melting tenderness she loved so much. "Well? What do you say to that, Doe-eyes?"

She looked at her ring. She looked at Cole, and she could almost hear the organ playing a wedding march and a host of angels singing joyful hosannas. Her smile right then could have lit the entire state of Virginia.

"I'd say I better hurry up and get to work designing wedding invitations," she answered, lifting her own fingers to trace a loving path over Cole's smiling lips, "because I think I'll be needing them in the very near future."

READ ABOUT THE AUTHOR

To meet Sheila Jamison, the heroine of THROUGH A GLASS DARKLY, is to know her creator, the irrepressible Sara Mitchell, who claims God in His wisdom blessed her with "an abundant sense of humor to compensate for my lapses of common sense and total lack of organization!" Like Sheila, Sara is warm, witty, sensitive, creative, lovable, and deliciously zany!

An Air Force wife, Sara has lived in many states. Wherever she is planted, she has found love to be the universal language and strangers are only friends whom she has not met, for she has 'the dubious propensity for rushing in where angels fear to tread in any group situation." Her zestful appreciation for God's plan for life and love have brought into being several unforgettable characters who will continue to delight you after many readings of this, her first romantic novel.

At this printing Sara resides with her husband, Phillip, and their two daughters, in Warner Robins, Georgia.

A Letter To Our Readers

Dear Reader:

Pioneering is an exhilarating experience, filled with opportunities for exploring new frontiers. The Zondervan Corporation is proud to be the first major publisher to launch a series of inspirational romances designed to inspire and uplift as well as to provide wholesome entertainment. In order that we might better contribute to your reading enjoyment, we would appreciate your taking a few minutes to respond to the following questions and return to:

> Editor, Serenade Books
> The Zondervan Publishing House
> 1415 Lake Drive, S.E.
> Grand Rapids, Michigan   49506

1. Did you enjoy reading THROUGH A GLASS DARKLY?

   ☐ Very much. I would like to see more books by this author!
   ☐ Moderately
   ☐ I would have enjoyed it more if _____

2. Where did you purchase this book? _____

3. What influenced your decision to purchase this book?

   ☐ Cover   ☐ Back cover copy
   ☐ Title   ☐ Friends
   ☐ Publicity   ☐ Other _____

4. Please rate the following elements from 1 (poor) to 10 (superior).

☐ Heroine   ☐ Plot
☐ Hero   ☐ Inspirational theme
☐ Setting   ☐ Secondary characters

5. Which settings would you like to see in future Serenade/Saga Books?

_____   _____

_____   _____

6. What are some inspirational themes you would like to see treated in future books?

_____   _____

_____   _____

7. Would you be interested in reading other Serenade/Serenata or Serenade/Saga Books?

☐ Very interested
☐ Moderately interested
☐ Not interested

8. Please indicate your age range:

☐ Under 18   ☐ 25–34   ☐ 46–55
☐ 18–24   ☐ 35–45   ☐ Over 55

9. Would you be interested in a Serenade book club? If so, please give us your name and address:

Name _____

Occupation _____

Address _____

City _____ State _____ Zip _____

Serenade Serenata Books are inspirational romances in contemporary settings, designed to bring you a joyful, heart-lifting reading experience.

Serenade Serenata books available in your local bookstore:

#1   ON WINGS OF LOVE, Elaine L. Schulte
#2   LOVE'S SWEET PROMISE,
     Susan C. Feldhake
#3   FOR LOVE ALONE, Susan C. Feldhake
#4   LOVE'S LATE SPRING, Lydia Heermann
#5   IN COMES LOVE, Mab Graff Hoover
#6   FOUNTAIN OF LOVE, Velma S. Daniels and
     Peggy E. King.
#7   MORNING SONG, Linda Herring
#8   A MOUNTAIN TO STAND STRONG,
     Peggy Darty
#9   LOVE'S PERFECT IMAGE, Judy Baer
#10 SMOKY MOUNTAIN SUNRISE,
     Yvonne Lehman
#11 GREENGOLD AUTUMN,
     Donna Fletcher Crow
#12 IRRESISTIBLE LOVE, Elaine Anne McAvoy
#13 ETERNAL FLAME, Lurlene McDaniel
#14 WINDSONG, Linda Herring
#15 FOREVER EDEN, Barbara Bennett
#16 THE DESIRES OF YOUR HEART,
     Donna Fletcher Crow
#17 CALL OF THE DOVE, Madge Harrah
#18 TENDER ADVERSARY, Judy Baer
#19 HALFWAY TO HEAVEN, Nancy Johanson
#20 HOLD FAST THE DREAM, Lurlene McDaniel
#21 THE DISGUISE OF LOVE, Mary LaPietra
#22 THROUGH A GLASS DARKLY, Sara Mitchell

Serenade Saga Books are inspirational romances in historical settings, designed to bring you a joyful, heart-lifting reading experience.

Serenade Saga books available in your local bookstore:

#1 SUMMER SNOW, Sandy Dengler
#2 CALL HER BLESSED, Jeanette Gilge
#3 INA, Karen Baker Kletzing
#4 JULIANA OF CLOVER HILL,
     Brenda Knight Graham
#5 SONG OF THE NEREIDS, Sandy Dengler
#6 ANNA'S ROCKING CHAIR,
     Elaine Watson
#7 IN LOVE'S OWN TIME,
     Susan C. Feldhake
#8 YANKEE BRIDE, Jane Peart
#9 LIGHT OF MY HEART, Kathleen Karr
#10 LOVE BEYOND SURRENDER,
     Susan C. Feldhake
#11 ALL THE DAYS AFTER SUNDAY,
     Jeanette Gilge
#12 WINTERSPRING, Sandy Dengler
 #13 HAND ME DOWN THE DAWN,
     Mary Harwell Sayler
#14 REBEL BRIDE, Jane Peart
#15 SPEAK SOFTLY, LOVE, Kathleen Yapp
#16 FROM THIS DAY FORWARD, Kathleen Karr
#17 THE RIVER BETWEEN, Jacquelyn Cook
#18 VALIANT BRIDE, Jane Peart
#19 WAIT FOR THE SUN, Maryn Langer

Watch for other books in the *Serenade Saga* series coming soon:

#20 KINCAID OF CRIPPLE CREEK, Peggy Darty
#21 LOVE'S GENTLE JOURNEY, Kay Cornelius